I0561890

CIRCLE OF WORDS

A Brussels Writers Circle anthology

Harvard Square Editions
New York
2016

ISBN 978-1-941861-21-9
Printed in the United States of America

Published in the United States by
Harvard Square Editions
www.harvardsquareeditions.org

ANTHOLOGY 2016

Alex Dampney "Circle of Words"

Table of Contents

Courtesy:

The Fun of Art

The majority of buyers of good books
Are other writers. It may be hard
To accept that this is true, but our planet

Is chock-a-block with successful,
Slow, fast or failed writers, plus
Writers *manqué,* writers-sure-to-be-

Famous-after-death, insane writers,
Those who call it something else,
Those who think it bad luck to own up

To their ambition, blocked writers
Who blather their books on bar stools,
Or those who play about with emotions

Of writing in the attics of their dreams,
Or who hope one day to be galvanised
By the possibility of simply making

Enough spare time to jot down the book
They have inside them, bobbing about
In their hearts, genitals, fingertips,

Or buried at the backs of their brains.
There are endless varieties of writers,
But the one thing common to them all

Is their generosity of spirit, willingness
To help each other, their fresh good looks,
Merry laughter and a disposition towards

Acts of shining, guileless virtue. Writers
Are a fine lot, but as readers every last
One of them has spasms of normality,

Though sometimes you really do need
To watch out for that slap on the back
And their overpraise. They feel for you

And tend to gild it a bit, and come on hot.
Afterwards, you pour yourself a glass of wine
And a bath. It's the main reward of the job.

—Kevin Ireland

Introduction

Hereby I summon all the Scribes of the world, in order to write what we feel:
From the Memory her whispers
From Poetry both her beauty and her sadness
From Love her pure essence...
Let's pave emptiness with Tales
Colour silence with rainbows
Rain with hope
Reconcile ourselves through Magic Words...
Such an Honour in a short period of life is a must.
Shall we all devote our energy and time to fight loneliness, stop hiding behind our pen-names, prejudices, power and glory, time and pessimism...
What are we but controverted humans, mortal beings endowed with wild hearts, in need of Muses, sweetness and fire?
The Circle of sensuous Ink offers immunity to tormented souls.
You are free to join. It is up to you.

—Océan Smets

Mauricio Ruiz

Memory

There's a light, a faint deflection of warmth
Not always
Though it feels like always
When I spring amid the yellow touch of laughter
Yours
Then mine
And it's in the mornings
That I feel a quiet, silky breeze
Though not always

Flowers, there, under the light
Breathing, singing of what once was.
Dusk, then night
But what has thus remained?

Kevin Dwyer

Rodeo Chameleon

What have you learned? What have you learned from your life with the lizard? What has it taught you to be kind to reptiles? Why, when they never gave anything back to you? How could you ever allow such insignificant life to be so entangled with yours?

It never changed color, it always remained a drab shade of green, no matter where it lay. They call it a natural defense mechanism. Green in the white cardboard box. Light green against the dark green plastic tree in the plastic habitat. Green even on the plastic brown rock that was included with the habitat to have a rock to scramble on. But it never scrambled. Kevin never once saw it move. It was the most patient and green thing. Almost as patient as that plastic rock. There was never any time to give it a name. It didn't make things easy, but he let it make them worse. Kevin was the yearning one in the couple, ever wanting from the lizard denying.

At the rodeo, under a circus tent in Billerica, there were boxes upon boxes of them, layered in a bigger box. The box was carried by the lizard hawker. Live chameleons. 99 cents. Clear plastic windows in each box allowed for a view of the lizards, all on display like a red-light district. The lizard hawker had one on his shoulder, on a leash. See them change color. Only 99 cents. He was intrigued, then covetous, and then he begged. Kevin made the solemn promises, this would be his. He hardly paid attention to the rodeo after that. It was straight from Texas. Clowns did stunts with hornless baby bulls. Broncos bucked and calves were roped. He had a chameleon now. He stared at it through the plastic window. It was his. He kept tapping the box. It never moved, not once, just the two heaving soft points on its sides that showed it was breathing.

Signs of life. The life of a chameleon. For 50 cents more, there was a box of live earthworms to feed it. He made the solemn promises. He looked into the box and fingered the white worms squirming in sawdust. How many would it eat? Where could he get more worms when these were gone? He put two of the worms in the box with the lizard right away. He wanted his chameleon to eat but most of all he wanted to see the life and death struggle pitting lizard against worm. It was natural, lizards ate earthworms, it wasn't cruel like what Bruce would do. Kevin wondered about such small bodies, inhabited by very small souls.

Earthworm destiny. Lizard destiny, linked now to the destiny of a 10-year-old boy. He did not know that the man, the man he called Bill who bought him the chameleon, was his father. This he would learn much, much later. Far too late for the lizard, far too late for Kevin, and far too late for it to matter. There was never even any time for a name. Kevin stared and poked, wanting it to do something, anything. The soft spots heaved. That's all it ever did.

After school the next day, from his own savings, he bought the lizard a habitat at Bradlees. 100% Plastic. Plastic trees. Plastic rocks. Plastic cactus. The cactus was primary green and designed with rivulets to retain water drops for the lizard to absorb through its skin when it rested on the plastic branches. Just like in nature on a real cactus. The live earthworms squirmed in the sawdust in their tiny box. None as of yet had been eaten. He began to wonder how he would keep the earthworms alive, for from the chameleon came none of the action he might have preferred from a pet. Kevin stared into the cage. The lizard stared out with one of its eyes, not seeming to see anything. Kevin was no doubt in its range of vision and sense. He wanted a current to pass between them, something meaningful, and something like trust, or companionship. Maybe he should have named it. He did not yet know about the dangers of too much yearning. And he never realized that he was scaring the thing to death, and death it would death.

One day later, the soft spots no longer heaved. Dead or alive, its appearance did not change, nor its color. This would be his rite of passage. For the first time. Something so close. Something he set out to take care of. His new pet. His too-late father's gift. His solemn promise. I'll take care of it. It's my responsibility. It has a soul, no matter how small. He owed it something. When Kevin left for school that day, it was on the cactus, maybe absorbing the water drops just like it said on the box. When he came home from school it was on the cactus, still. What did his mother think, spending the day alone in the house with the lizard? He opened the lid and pried the chameleon gently from the cactus. It was no longer afraid. He held its cold, dry corpse in his palms with outstretched arms. The lizard was so light. It was near Easter, time of death and hope. Tears flooded his cheeks. He walked like a mummy into his mother's room. She looked up from her TV show, couldn't figure it out. Her son bleating and sobbing, holding out the dead lizard. She must have been startled. Her comfort was of little solace to him. He alone knew. The grief was all his. Maybe he had to seek that solace elsewhere. She thought it odd that he wept so for a lizard.

So this, this, would be his first funeral. They didn't let him go to Grandpa's. They said he was too young. He would do this on his own terms. His tears would be for the lizard, for all the loss, for all the moments they would never share. Not for the now-buried grandfather he visited at a nursing home, struck with Alzheimer's, yet perhaps still knowing certain things. That's why he bared his teeth, reminding Kevin that we are all monkeys. They pulled Kevin out of the room fast. Perhaps they thought that at the funeral, maybe-Grandpa would try to bite him again. Kevin was ready now, ready to get closer to death, ready to know about the things they kept from children. Adults try to shelter children so much from it, but children find it anyway. They know it is there.

Some even seek it out. Some even make it happen. Bruce was a specialist, taking Kevin many times on the long march of death, holding matches to caterpillars, and picking off grasshoppers' legs – from hundreds' caught and kept in jars along with slugs, caterpillars, crickets and salamanders- and placing its helpless body in the path of a colony of red ants. They would watch for hours at a time, commenting on its slow death throes. For some reason Bruce was kind to salamanders. He found them intelligent and graceful, deserving of life and his mercy. When Bruce's mother died, he went to her funeral. Bruce knew exactly who his father was, a butcher who brought home the best cuts every day.

Death is all around, all around, and the children know it.

They even make it happen. Kevin had failed the lizard, but he would not fail its funeral. He took his mother's big cooking spoon from the kitchen drawer. The one she used to scoop ice cream and to serve up a boiled dinner. The one with which she would serve him dinner that very evening. It was also the American chop suey spoon. He gathered a few popsicle sticks in the back of the drawer and grabbed some twisty-ties. He still had the box it came in, the long rectangular box, with probably just enough room for the lizard to turn around in. The guy at the rodeo had one on his shoulder on a little leash. It didn't move either. Maybe it too was dead now. Kevin lined the box with fluffy cotton and lay the lizard carcass in the makeshift casket. He stared at it through the window. As in life, it failed to move. He zipped everything up in the pockets of his Bradlee's parka. He didn't tell his mother where he was going. She had seen him cry the night before. She assumed he was over it.

He had seen enough funerals on television to know what to do. Choosing a gravesite was not difficult. The second he knew the lizard was dead, it came to him immediately. He had been there many times before. It was a recluse wooded area, almost across the street from his complex, tucked in between a disused parking garage, a bus stop on Cummins Highway, and a shopping strip featuring the Bradlee's where he bought the lizard habitat. The kind of place that only kids find. So secluded yet with signs of life everywhere, in shreds and pieces, nothing no longer as it was. Makeshift or not, what is a cemetery if not a dump? Clots of toilet paper clung to the barren tree branches in a mockery of Christmas at Easter. Bottles and cans littered the ground in various states of disarray and decay. Broken glass lay everywhere, labels here and there holding together some of the pieces, still readable with words like Schlitz, Pabst, High Life. It had been a refuge for some. Shreds of magazines lie strewn on the ground in patches. Body parts on the shreds, images, a bare thigh, a bare breast. Right across the street, looking over to Cummins Highway, was a real cemetery, a human cemetery, the Forest Hills Cemetery. He learned later, over thirty years later, much too later, that his own grandmother, his real grandmother, his mother's mother, was buried there. If he had only known. His mother never told him because she never wanted him to start scouring the graves, looking at the dates. Dates mattered to her. He never understood why. So many were the places kept in the shadows from him. So many were the things he was not allowed to know. And now, a stone's throw from the grave of the unknown grandmother, a chameleon lies. Good enough for a lizard, some would say.

It was early spring, around Easter. Kevin made his way off the sidewalk onto the worn patch that lead up to a passage through thick sprouting bush to the wooded area. Crooking his neck, not far off behind him, across the dog-leg of American Legion Highway, he could see his own bedroom window through the grid of the fire escape. That was where the lizard had lived and died. That was where, years later, together with his brother, he picked his mother up from the floor after a fall when she was sick. Her still body would lie there too. Did it really matter what was written on a tombstone? Or where we place them?

The spot was as far in the middle of the trees as possible. He could see the old 5-gallon paint can full of used motor oil where Bruce would drop crickets and invite Kevin to watch them writhe, sinking in the black oil. Kevin began turning up the earth with the spoon. No need for six feet under. He dug a hole three times as deep as the box. He placed it gently in the bottom of the hole and contemplated the sight. He knew that he wasn't acting normally. He knew that a flush down the toilet would have, and should have, done the trick.

This would be his rite of passage. They denied him his grandfather's funeral. No one would do that for him, so he would do it himself. This is what he yearned for, and this is the death ritual that he would have. It was his life and his death. He scooped the freshly dug earth into the opening. It didn't really have that sound, the one he heard in the movies, of earth hitting the casket. His eyes swelled, but he remained deliberate and solemn as he pressed down the earth. After the box was buried, he fashioned a cross from the popsicle sticks that his mother always saved in the kitchen drawer. What was a funeral without a cross, even for the lowliest creatures? He steadied the cross in the earth above the grave and formed a mound around it for support. He stayed on his knees and admired his work. No words for the soul of the lizard came to him. So he rocked as he wept true tears of grief, thrashing at the chest, alone among the trees, the toilet paper, the scraps of porn magazines strewn on the now-hallowed ground, a place he had been to before and where he would return.

*

"Let's dig it up. Let's see the body. I bet you it rotted."

Bruce was two years older, two years smarter, two years more callous, two years more malevolent. Kevin took Bruce to the exact spot. He undug the grave on Bruce's command. Kevin didn't know how to say no to Bruce. The box was still white, a soiled white. It was then that he wished he had named it. He wanted to call out to it. To apologize. He knew what Bruce would want to do. He knew that Bruce would want to dig the grave up. To pick the thing up by its tail. To wag it in his face. To burn it just to see how fast it would burn. To watch its body curl under the heat. To put it on the road and watch cars run it over. To feed the carcass to red ants.

"Open it. Let's see."

Kevin dusted off the box. His fingertip traced the lizard's head visible through the window, just as he left it. His mind raced before Bruce's challenge. He couldn't think of a way to defy Bruce. He wanted to kick and thrash out. Why did he have to care so much? A toilet flush would have done the trick. Rituals are so vulnerable. Kevin looked up. Over Bruce's shoulder, across Cummins Highway, he could see Mount Calvary Cemetery. His grandmother was buried there, but he didn't know it at the time. Lies were all around him. Deception never has limits, lies before you as lies behind you. Holding the sacred box in his hand, he turned and raced down the hill, never before behaving so insolently to Bruce's dominance. Kevin was far ahead before Bruce ever thought of giving chase. He would never talk to Bruce again.

He entered furtively, his mother was right there at the door. He would have preferred to go straight to his room.

"Alright Kev?"

"Yeah, I was with Bruce."

"You're looking funny, you alright?"

"Yeah, Ma, I took the stairs all the way up, s'all."

Kevin made for his 6th floor bedroom and let some time

go by. He looked out through the rusting fire escape as the room darkened. The box was on his desk. There were cemeteries out there. There were cemeteries everywhere. A flush down the toilet would do it.

Eyes

People on the streets
All of passion created
Eyes to the pavement

Elements

It's so warm she said
Aching whisper running deep
You found the right spot

Baby breath

Passion created
Liquid eyes and baby breath
And all that is left

Drops

Drops out of nowhere
Become gushes and showers
Drench skin and limb

Embrace

Shadow in the fog
Calling yesterday's lover
Embrace me now

Post (with Tanka variation)

Warmth swells and lingers
Following gush and glisten
No thoughts no motion
(Hot breath voiceless the dark
A shudder spreading ripples)

Black Holes

You came on the scene
Saying pretty things about your pretty life
You told me about strawberry dreams
And all the things you like
You told me everything
But there were black holes in your mind

There were times when I thought
We'd find a place to settle down
I saw two cups of coffee
A spotted dog and the fuzzy brown
Never thinking of the black holes
The black holes in your mind

Falling angels
Have no time to scream and shout
A life worth living
Is a life worth talking about
Yet you said nothing
Nothing about the black holes in your mind

Some have said
Why don't you just walk out the door
But they don't know
The reasons that I came here for
Stuck between you and the black holes
The black holes in your mind

So here we are
In the prison of your mind
It's not about how you live
But about what you leave behind
Here in the black holes
The black holes of your mind

Too many lies too many black holes
Too many tears too many black holes
So much time so many black holes
So much fear so many black holes
Stuck between you and the black holes of your mind

Oasis
I thought there was an oasis in the desert of your heart
But you just made me come here to watch it all dry up
I travelled far into the depths created for our dreams

And found a hard and bitter core depleted of all aim
Time begins and time ends and lizards crawl about
They don't know what sunset means and forget what
they've been taught
The cactus slowly sucks the life from the fleeting morn
Never minding never caring for a love forlorn
Call me callous call me kind call me Ishmael
Cast away upon the shore a shipwreck as my cell
In the desert of your heart I do lay me down
And together we fall asleep in our shelter from the storm

In a neither world we are
Neither here neither there
Neither seeing neither being
Neither into neither been to
Neither soul neither sea
Neither you neither me
In a neither world we are

I Just Say OK

Before darkness gets the better of me
Before the need takes over
I must confess I'm of the breed
To blind my eyes forever
To see the sights to dream a dream
Ecstasy won't do it
There's got to be hypocrisy
Or else we won't get through it

A symphony appears to me

But I just turn away
Eternity shines like the sea
And I just say OK

Before going blind maybe I should see
The mistakes are all my own
The darkness now's engulfing me
From sadness I'm immune
To dream away perchance to sleep
Is all that glitters gold?
Tomorrow cries I'm here you see
On that we've all been sold

The queen extends her crown to me
But I just turn away
A fleeting opportunity
And I just say OK

Océan Smets

Wind Flower

A Huron Chief offered me a large feather headdress. It was only then that I realized I belonged to a lost tribe: White Feather was born.

I used to spend most of my time in his tepee, made from buffalo skin. I enjoyed wearing his *wampum* necklace with my boxers, writing nonstop. Words had been nestling in my bones long before I left my amniotic bag. That goddam novel did not allow me to rest, night and day. It tortured my mind trying to flow. I was its slave for a couple of winters in the Grand Nord.

Wind Flower's warmth appeased my soul. He never labelled or tried to change me, neither did he ask me anything in return. I could breathe, felt free to swim, laugh and love. He tried hard to make me happy, adoring me from the distance, respecting my wishes, dreams and priorities. The trout he fished for breakfast was finally accepted.

He slept me in his arms when I had a nightmare, singing a Huron lullaby, because the dreamcatcher never worked for me. He knew who I really was.

Life stood still, stood by, but for how long? Ocean waves were still waiting to beat, double rainbows kept hiding behind the clouds (wishing another destiny?).

The past is a long conversation, a place of memory carpeted with fall. This is why today, eight years later, I long to go back to Wendake, to spend some Moons with my Huron tribe.

I miss Wind Flower, mostly his spirituality. I am eager to embrace him, to swim with him in the icy water. He is my hero. He painted the rainbow again centuries ago. He knows how to spread his wings on my scars. His peace of mind creates in my dreams a silent oasis, of balance and harmony. He wakes up in me with the caress of a feather. He wakes up in me the being that I hide.

He is mentally agile, able to go from the outer world to the inner one, penetrating the moment, and flying through the air. His energy is anchored in earth, yet it reaches infinity. He can communicate with himself and the others, drawing new movements that he teaches me while we dance. He makes my heart beat, although he can make it stop voluntarily.

Wendake: Huron reservation in Jeune-Lorette, Quebec, Canada.

Janus and Kalajaan

Both of them were created in the same spring, and enjoyed rather a reasonable life, that had lasted for about two hundred and fifty years.

Whether they were twins, friends or simply close relatives remained only a technicality in their minds. They matched, were good partners and shared great expectations. They helped each other in their privileged job of bringing to perfection the last generation of intelligent robots.

When Janus stared at his/her companion, his/her sensor cells slowed down, s/he could then filter odd waves. No outer noise interfered. Those were precious seconds in his/her peaceful existence. Unspoken messages reached his/her artificial skin. Among them s/he could decode most. Yet something unexplainable was missing.

Kalajaan aroused contradictory feelings. S/He could become tense or excited in microns, or drastically lower energy, but her/his speed was regular.

All they had been longing for was giving birth to a human creature. It was their deepest wish. For ages this act had been impossible to materialize. A long life expectancy could perhaps enable them, brilliant genetic engineers. The right alternance of chromosomes and the precise DNA chains, together with artificial insemination, might eventually be the clue.

Be that as it may, they had to run the risk. Therefore, they started to gather old books from the early two thousands. Some attempts were infertile, but little by little they deciphered the old biology treatises. These beings were hybrid units, sexed and mortal.

Their extinction was by all means predictable. The earth had collapsed after countless germ wars. The extraterrestrial baby should therefore have his/her genes manipulated. Therapy had to be used to prevent social conflicts.

On the ninth moon Janus was required at the Cyber-Lab: the task had been accomplished: Jai was born. Crying in his stellar cradle, he would find comfort with them.

Kalajaan viewed them smugly. They threw all the documents into the incinerator. No one would ever know their secret.

Northward

Northward is the land where greyish skies prolong the winter, foretell my home and overturn my feelings, somewhere far from golden or volcanic sands.

Still the poetaster in exile, sensing beyond a doubt, can expect very seldom from a special moon an inspiring night.

"Be daring", coerces the canvas behind the cloth and I, in the moonlight here, as Helena sleeps tight.

Now, when I am at my best, and perhaps at all times, my insights remind me of my studio in Brussels. That is where I belong, in my heart, which is where I want to be. There, nothing prevents communication. It is home to many tales, but also to a certain sadness.

It won't kill part of me to move elsewhere. Who would I be in the next years? I would then feel the absence of desire as its meaning had been irrevocably transformed.

Woman

On the snow flakes,
On the Grand Place,
On the dreams,
I write your name.

Sarah R. Harris

The Legacy

I lag behind a group of great aunts clutching handbags,
billowing like laundered sheets,
as confident as shining spoons.
They form an avenue of wrinkled oaks
providing source and shelter,
standing firm against the ravages of storm and time.

It is unthinkable that they should disappear
along with mackintoshes, peppermints in tins.
Their houses crumbling, their gardens overgrown,
their lawns amok with moss.

What have they left?
A scattering of flimsy shrubs,
reluctant to take root, liable to blow away.
Though long since adult,
still not grown-up enough
to nurture seedlings,
carry on the task.

For years I thought they'd gone completely.
Nothing in my life resembled theirs.
But today I find their shoes upon my feet

and hear their words inside my head.
I recognize their turn of phrase
and look around, surprised,
to find them smiling at me in the mirror,
that line of staunch, strong ladies,
going back through generations.
How long, I ask, have you been here?
All the time, they say.

C.S. Begu

The Spy

Raw nature. That's how it looked from this side of the hill all the way North towards the peaks. Not sunny, not colorful, but joyful nonetheless. The joy of the unexplored forest, brimming with hidden life and the long treks of brother Giorgos, every afternoon at two o'clock. All against the advice of the Romanian monks, who keep warning him of brown bears roaming about in search of raspberries. But he never, ever listens! One of these days this will end in one big drama.

But Brother Giorgos' curiosity seems to surpass his fear. He was raised to take the path of a celibate monk, spending the last seven years among the torched cliffs of Holy Mount Athos in Northern Greece. He had been dying to go somewhere wild and fresh—at least that's what people have been saying about him. And since he was finally permitted to settle here at Frasinei Monastery, in the shadow of the temperate Romanian Carpathians, he is said to be fascinated with the dramatic change in the seasons. That's why he takes long trips by himself into the backwoods of the monastery, carrying a crooked staff as both climbing aid and defense. The bishop from Valcea, who often visits, says he strikes him as Moses in Exodus with the notable difference that nobody would follow him for fear of the wildlife. The bishop. Always poking fun at the monks.

Brother Giorgos walked through the woods with serene confidence, as a monarch surveying his domain, able to spot any flaws in the scenery. And, though sporting a long, unkempt beard, ragged monk habit and a cold demeanor (despite his being Greek and all that) Brother Giorgos looked absolutely beautiful...

But Sister Eleonora checked herself. Such thoughts were going against her vows. Crossing herself three times and kissing her holy beads, she started to crawl back from the edge of the bluff, overseeing the back of the strict monastery, where not even female animals were allowed. She took one more look at the young monk, starting on his usual exploration tours. Helping himself up the incline with his royal staff, he followed the animal trail, out of the meadow and into the forest.

As Sister Eleonora accepted her fate once more, she turned her gaze away with a sigh. But before she left the edge of the hill, she turned for one last time. Her eyes searched across the valley, but only met the empty path entering the forest, leaving behind a lonely meadow. With fingers intertwined below her chin, she pleaded to the Heavens: "My Lord, I beg you, keep the bears off!"

Picnic on the White Cliff

With the back of his hand, Daniel wiped the chicken wing grease around his lips. He then walked to the edge of the cliff and started throwing stones in the Olt river reservoir beyond the road, far below. *Bloop, once. Bloop, twice...*

He enjoyed coming here with his older brother and his friends from North Quarter. They would barbecue, wrestle for football cards and admire the Olt Valley, snaking its way north through the motionless army of Carpathian ogres, into Transylvania. Everything was perfectly arranged as in a scenic post-card promoting the Garden of Eden. And, after what had happened today, Daniel could not feel more like in Heaven.

That morning, back at the school gym, Coach Barbu chose him to be the captain for the next season. He felt the luckiest boy in the world. But not because this would make him more popular. He knew the opposite would happen -- they would all envy him, like he had envied Dacian, the outgoing captain. Not because he'd get better grades -- that doesn't make you very cool even if the teachers do decide to give you a pass. No. The reason why Daniel felt this surge of anticipation was that, as captain, he had received the key to the gym supply room. And tomorrow, after school, that supply room is going to be the best thing that ever happened to him and Elena. Finally.

The chalk cliff reigned over the reservoir. Far on the other side, the town was a thin, white line drawn along the ancient Roman road, against a background of foothills. It looked lonely and awkward, dwarfed by forested creatures with scales made of trees in various nuances of summer. Capela Ridge, flanking the town from the West was a giant crocodile, resting after a good meal of sunshine.

Bloop, a third time. Bloo.

The ground shuddered under his feet. His legs tensed, resisting the presentiment. He turned around with a tremor, ready for the jump back. But the silent scream of the chasm paralyzed him -- as it had happened in a dream, just a few nights ago. In a trance, he started gliding towards the abyss, along with a brittle patch of soil covering the lip of the bluff.

Twenty meters below, his eyes caught a glimpse of the dark asphalt, heated by a productive summer sun. A few pillow-sized boulders plunged ahead, as if to prepare his sleeping quarters.

The grass rustled nearby. His brother launched into a suicidal leap and Daniel was caught, just as he was going over the edge. But now he felt himself slipping away, his hand greasy from the chicken wings. For a moment he looked into his brother's eyes, knowing. The inevitable rendered them mute.

It was over. No hope left. He was already mid-fall, his brother's howl of anguish piercing the serenity of the valley. He tried to claw his way into the rock wall, but it was pointless. Kicking the air with his hands and legs, he could do nothing but wait for the impact. It came.

But not before Daniel could ask himself: "Wh..."

On the Shifting Path

I am strolling down on the beach at peace with myself, while a sweet-and-salty breeze is feeding me with optimism and tolerance. Further down the coast beams the five-star hotel. It's built for celebrities, double-dealing politicians and the occasional businessman cheating on his wife. Inside, shuffling like termites in a fresh nest, an assortment of brown-nosed waiters, doormen, room-servicers, janitors, clerks and their slick managers are sucking up to the guests. Those numbskulls.

Breathing in, breathing out. At peace, please!

The beach is splattered with butts, legs, breasts and chests, changing positions to receive their allotted share of sunlight. I am treading ahead barefoot, my nose feeding on the breezes, with sandals swinging in my hands, following the narrow part of the beach where sea and shore have been meeting since the beginnings of the Earth. Here, on this ever-shifting path, I get the best of both worlds. Now I'm in the sea, now I'm on land. In the sea, on land. Sea, land...

But the sea reacts. The regular waves morph into malignant shapes, bulging out of gravity's mold and boiling over my path. Before I have time to run away, the sea surrounds me, while the sand gives in beneath me grain by grain. Soon enough I find myself knee-deep, then chest-deep, then mouth-deep in the gargling masses of salty water. The insatiable sea is stealing more and more land from the dry world.

And all the sunbathing butts, legs, breasts and chests start scampering around in the fertile foams, colliding in a havoc of screams and splashes on what just a few minutes earlier had been a serene and peaceful beach.

The waters are now above my eyes. Despite my attempt to swim back to solid ground, where you can stand, breathe and pass judgement on doormen, celebrities, politicians, and businessmen who cheat on their wives, the far depths of the sea have already hooked me, reeling me in. And away the sea takes me, and the waves start to fight amongst each other for their prey.

Gone is the safety of the shifting path, on the edge of the water, where I felt protected both from the menacing depths of the sea and from the back-stabbing joviality of the populated land.

To The Stone Bull Bluff

There was something prancing around in the woods of my childhood. I had felt it those late nights when we would all gather, pick up some homemade liquor and climb the hill up to Stone Bull Bluff, in the pitch black of midnight.

We were many, so the dread of being alone at night in a dark forest was masked by our loud chattering and the twinkling of our cigarettes. We were many and we were men.

The climb took an hour, but once you got there you enjoyed the view of the sleeping town sketched out by the rows of street lamps lining the main boulevard and contoured by the Dam signal beacons to the North. It was worth it.

I was last, stumbling up the violent slopes, grasping for patches of grass to pull myself up, trying to catch up with the group. At times, when they went around shrubs a little too fast or over mounds a little too quickly, I found myself in absolute loneliness, in the dark open space. Nothing was standing between me and Evil. I realized then that the fear of being alone is not about loneliness at all. It is the fear of another. Because everything you hear, you actually feel attacking you from behind. You look up, but there's nothing there but the jaundiced stars, flickering some light on you through hand-shaped oak branches, cracking in the gentle night winds. They have become your ambassadors, pleading to the heavens for mercy.

But the anguish retreats back into the bushes—you're safe. You're with friends. And you are many. And you are men.

Onore

Tony smiled bitterly. His brother Paulie and his ten-year-old daughter Laura were standing there, on the front porch, when, suddenly, the girl darted toward Tony. She just could not wait to greet him, her favorite uncle. To this Tony did not know how to react.

Paulie wiped the gloom off his face and set up a welcome smile. Tony gave him a quick glance, then tossed his jaw upwards into an old Italian *saluto*. Paulie understood.

"Laura, *cara mia*. Leave Uncle Tony alone! You're bothering him. Go back inside! Come on, go back inside"

Tony dropped to one knee and started to caress Laura's dark hair.

"No. No. It's OK, P. How is *la mia piccola principessa*?"

"Hey, Tone! Come on! Laura, come to Daddy."

Paulie came rushing down on the porch steps and grabbed Laura with a powerful hug, getting lost in the embrace.

"Daddy! You're hurting me!"

"Daddy's so sorry. But you know Daddy loves you very much, no?"

"Uhuuuh. And I love daddy too" she smiled, the benevolent angel, willing to forgive and forget.

"Now, you be a good little girl and wait inside, OK? Your Uncle Tony and I will be back soon. Right, Tone?"

"Right, P."

They both said goodbye to Laura and then walked to the car, parked further up on the street, where their good friend Al was waiting for them. He got out of the passenger seat, greeted Paulie and then moved into the back seat, leaving the front seat for Tony's brother. Before entering the car Paulie looked back at the house. Laura was already up at her bedroom window, cheering them on their ride. He waved to her, then he got in and turned to the two men.

"Come on, guys! Can't you talk to him again? Al?"

"Sorry, Paulie. You know how it is..."

"What about you, Tone?"

Tony avoided his brother's pleading eyes and instead he looked the other way, but right there in the middle of the street was Laura's hopscotch, chalked in blue with yellow numbers. The drawing filled his chest with unbearable ache. Maybe he could still do something. Maybe if he sells his club and pays the underboss he could make up for Tony's screw up.... And then maybe, just maybe...

But Paulie's loud breathing jolted him back to reality. He knew all too well nothing could be done. The club is not even actually his, no matter how you cut it. Besides, this whole thing ain't about the money, it's about fucking *onore*. And what a curse that is.

"Look P., you love Laura, right?"

"More than anything, Tone. You know that," said Paulie with a glimmer of fading hope.

"And I love her too, P. And that's exactly why we can't try anything. Al and I talked all about it. We can't get stupid."

Head down in a prayerful posture, Paulie stretched his palms on the dashboard, taking long breaths to calm himself, blinking rapidly and tapping his fingers on the black plastic, trying to squeeze a way out. He nodded his head left and right a couple of times in revolt. But then he started nodding his head up and down. He gave in.

"Yeah, Tone. You're right. I guess you're right. Did you get to talk to Rose?"

"Yeah, P. Rose agreed. She's...She's OK with it. It's all fine. Laura will be taken good care of."

"And what about Laura? What will you tell her?"

Tony started the Cadillac and put it into "Drive". He pushed the gas pedal and the car pulled away slowly through the serene Jersey suburb.

"I got no idea, P. No idea. But, don't you worry. I'll think of something. I promise you I will."

Alex Dampney

Unravelling

You're bound in knots, not knowing what to do
your head is reeling, filled with twisted cords
that tie your brain and stop you thinking true,
long strings of words coiled fast and stored.
There is no straight, just loops and tangled strands
of wire wool and ageing unbrushed hair
that lie in wait for someone's dextrous hand
to coax them, gently tease them, from their lair.

Your friends are here, bright beacons in the night.
Approaching us is hard for you. You back
off as bloody teeth of distrust bite,
and keep away, your tangled threads intact.

Oh weeping child, don't cry despair, keep faith.
Until you're ready, we'll be here, we'll wait.

Through the Pane of Glass

Through the pane of glass
I see my mother in the kitchen.
My sister on her lap, body
tensed, feet kicking,

tears streaming down her face,
she's recounting a disaster
of how others called her names.

Through the pane of glass
the sun lights up the faces
of my mother and my sister,
whose tears turn to laughter
and my sister feels so safe
in my mother's warm embrace.

Through the pane of glass
a joke is being shared.
She's standing on a chair
stirring pots upon the stove.
My mother's eyes are soft.

Through the pane of glass
the air grows thick with steam.
The kitchen's warm and cosy.
I shiver, looking in.

Through the pane of glass
My mother can not see
me standing in the rain.

Through the pane of glass
the images have blurred

through the pane

Closet World (Villanelle)

A shrouded cupboard, caked with dirt and smears
containing truths a family hid away
has been ignored for more than thirty years.

This closet world encases secret fears
where terror-stricken creatures often pray.
In a shrouded cupboard, caked with dirt and smears

volcanoes spew out dust and lava sears
young skins submerged in boiling mud, where they
have been ignored for more than thirty years.

A flooding basin holds the bloody tears
of wounded beasts that roam in disarray.
In a shrouded cupboard, caked with dirt and smears

a girl hears screeches, harsh against her ears.
She knows the dread of night without a day,
she's been ignored for more than thirty years.

She stands and stares. Her trembling body hears
the screaming monsters trapped and locked away
in a shrouded cupboard, caked with dirt and smears
that's been ignored for more than thirty years

Nick C. Hogg

Bird of Passage

To Aneta
This town sees them all,
People here for work, here for love,
Here to hide, here to seek
But, of them all,
The true adventurer is you:
The bird of passage.

You left your home,
The place comfort
Comes easiest
In soft familiarity,
For a snatch of life
Beyond safe bounds
Aware how your nest
Cannot be fully feathered
Without those things
That can only come from far away.

You flew in with the warmth and colour
Of the land you left behind.
For you a base on which to build
For each of us, the treat

Of gradual enrichment.

Bright sparkling bird,
You rekindled a perspective,
For many of us dimmed,
Of what our reality means
In the wider scheme of things.

Here you built yourself a microlife
Encapsulated by a macroexistance
And held so very tight.

Now the ring around this experience
Bound to evaporate in time
As the knowledge you've acquired
Oozes out to influence
How you see and judge and think
In years to come.

You put down virtual roots
Perhaps you thought
They'd be easy to dissolve.
Have you perhaps seen how
They have encircled and entwined
The very fabric of the place.
Removing them, as you must,
Cannot but cause pain. Yours the
Pain of going back, of going forward.
Ours the pain of staying still
And watching.

You worked so hard

For your satisfaction here
Foreign climes, familiar dreams
Important here, vital there
You were always anchored in yourself
You did reach out and now can fly
The homeward route, job done
Like a bird of passage.
To the nest of which
You came, to touch us all,
Each in a different way
With your youth and your enthusiasm.

So dear Anya, the adventure's done
Ant it's a fabulous win for all.
You will take us with you
Just as you will stay with us.

Kathleen M. Reding

Euphoria

A dream?
Really was it?
I am not sure.
I want to keep it.
The feeling is leaving.
Please don't go.
Hold on.
Stay

Possession

Not possible.
Leave me alone.
I need my liberty.
You must go your way.
I will miss you.
Please go now.
What a relief.
Freedom

Sarah Strange

Enter - Philip I

It's been hot and sultry for a week
The sun begins to bronze my feet
All my jackets left behind
For once the weather has been kind.

We reach the 21st this year
In blazing sunshine; it is clear
That our modest black-red-yellow nation
Will undergo a transformation.

King Albert, the second of the name,
Has for some time made it plain
That the affairs of State should be
In the hands of a younger man than he.

Forced by Baudouin's death in Spain
In Ninety-Three, he's learnt to reign;
Kept Belgium on an even keel
An act requiring nerves of steel.

The pessimists who expect "*la drache*"
To pour cold water on the bash
As Philip steps up to the mark
 Might have, for once, a change of heart.

Filip/Philippe – how will he sign?
It's a language question every time!
But with his lovely wife Mathilde
The succession at least is fulfilled.

R.I.P. Ann

It is late, pooled darkness on my desk
Electricity does its best
To play the role of day prolonged
But Night and all its shades are strong.

It's at such moments one is prey
To darker thoughts which find a way
To strut unbidden on our stage
And force us to turn back the page.

I think of Friday; sad surprise
An unpredictable demise
Of a lady writer, colleague, friend
Who for many years would spend

Time with other literary folk
On varied writings – all bespoke!
We saw her last two weeks ago
She smiled goodnight; we could not know

This fleeting glance would be our last
Life's like that – people just drift past
Our minds cling onto them a while
Recalling them with saddened smile ...
18.08.2014

Jaroslav Albert

Jesus Unchained

Mr. Tarantino entered the studio that morning looking exceptionally pleased. As all evil geniuses eventually do, he'd grown tired of making pictures that come second nature to him and decided some weeks back he was going to write and direct a "serious" film – no Tarantino stuff -- one that will leave the critics gasping for adjectives as they click away at those fresh Tomatoes. He even hired theatrical actors who, he believed, would give his film a more dramatic overtone; never mind that they had not been trained in stunt choreography. But such a feat had not come easy; for the past week he'd been in a rut, trying to figure out how and where he might inject some action into what he perceived thus far to be a stale piece of bunk. That is -- until today.

Quentin passed the security and checked in his cell phone. His producer saw him and was coming over.

"Hey Julie," he greeted her from afar, having just downed a sip of the best goddamn coffee in town.

Julie, a nerdy-looking chick with glasses, threw her arms open in bewilderment, holding the new script. "What are you doing?" she asked.

"What?"

"This," Julie raised the script to his face.

"Oh, yeah, isn't it great?"

Julie did not answer.

"You don't like it?"

Of course she liked it -- he *was* her boss -- but that was not the issue. "You can't just rewrite the script last minute," she said.

"I had to."

"You had to?"

"Yeah, I felt the hero was too...you know, not very heroic," Quintin explained.

"Not very heroic? Jesus? He saved all humanity."

Quentin squinted (a gesture which earned him the nickname "Squintin' Quentin") and his face grimaced. "Yeah, I'm not sure I get how that's heroic. I mean, didn't he sacrifice himself to himself so he himself could forgive everyone else's sins?"

Julie did not look pleased.

"Look, I know you're into that whole born again thing, and that's great. I just don't think my audience will perceive being flogged, hung by the wrists, dying and doing nothing to punish the motherfuckers who did that to you as heroic. That's why I want Jesus to 'die' (he gestured quotations) in the middle of the film so that in the second half he can—"

"But Quentin," Julie interrupted, "the actors have already learned their parts."

"Oh, don't even sweat that, it'll be fine. Besides, there's not much talking in the new part." Quentin then clapped his hands, turning his attention to the cast. "Okay, let's roll. Why don't we move to the scene where Jesus – where is he, by the way? There you are. What's your name again?"

The actor playing Jesus timidly stepped up to the great director and replied: "John, sir."

"Okay, John, here's what I want you to do. I want you to

take these Kamas – or as I call them, sickles – and..."

John took the weapons in his hands and looked horrified.

"Is there a problem?"

"Well, sir...I'm supposed to play Jesus," John said.

"You are. You are! You just came back from the dead, although you didn't actually die – your disciples stole your body and revived you. I mean, you *were* dead, but only clinically. You understand? Well, now it's a month later and you got your strength back. And you're angry, and when I say angry, I mean you're pissed out of your wits at these motherfucken' Rabbis; you're gonna wipe out the entire Sanhedrin; you're gonna storm in –" and as he explained, Mr. Tarantino slashed through the air with his hands. "— and then camera three will zoom in on your face, which will have these brooks of blood rolling down -- just the way you looked when you were on the cross. It'll have revenge written all over it. Just awesome."

After a moment of reflexion on his genius, Quentin clapped his hands and told everyone to get ready. The seventy one priests to be slaughtered took their places in the court. Jesus hid behind the door.

"Okay John," Quentin yelled out through his megaphone, "when I say action, you kick the door down and...and do your thing."

"My thing, sir?" John said.

"Okay, here we go. And...action!"

The door flew off the hinges as if blown up by a grenade. Jesus stepped inside. The priests looked shocked. Then, he began slashing left and right.

"Cut, cut, cut..."

Quentin walked up to John, raised his hands to ear

level, squinted, grimaced, and tilted his head and said: "Here's the thing…John." And while trying to emulate John's performance, he explained: "when you do this, for example, it doesn't look like you're actually hurting anyone. You see what I mean? You need to really wanna kill the guy, and go at it, too…but just miss him by an inch or so. Got it? Okay, let's go again. We start after the door is kicked in."

The actors got set. Silence. "And action!"

Jesus threw himself at the Rabbis. And the Rabbis, seeing how seriously he'd taken to following Mr. Tarantino's instructions, began, quite randomly, to disperse, many going off camera.

"Cut, cut, cut, cut, *cut*. What the hell was that? You're in a room, surrounded by walls, okay – if you run off the camera, to the viewer, you're moving through walls. And John…" Quentin walked up to Jesus again. "John…okay, let me explain this from a slightly different angle. Have you seen Kill Bill volume one and two?"

"Yes, sir, it was advised to me that I watch all your--"

"Great. Excellent, that's very good, John. Now imagine you're Uma without the yellow," and he looked John up and down and made sort of a face, "never mind that – just imagine your Uma, clad, very clad, and then imagine the chief rabbi as Lucy Liu and the rest of the lot as the crazy eighty eight. Okay? Got it?"

"I think so, sir, but—"

"Awesome! Let's roll!"

Cameras set, actors in place, Jesus armed. "And…action!"

And Jesus went off on a rampage, rabbis fell, blood everywhere, and the great Quentin Tarantino was finally satisfied.

T.D. Arkenberg

Hollywood Calls

Hollywood. The word triggers a kaleidoscope of images—
movies, magic, star power—a place where fortunes are
made... and lost. A summons to the land of dreams filled me
with excitement. But judgment of my first major foray into
writing sobered the high. After letting corporate America
define me for over two decades, I turned to writing for
purpose. Fiction had always been a passion, but grasping
rungs of the corporate ladder and trying to hold on for dear
life consumed my energy. Once free to write, worry gripped
me. Could left brain relinquish its dominion?   More
importantly, could right brain, as atrophied as a withered
appendage, grow strong?

I'd just finished an early draft of my debut novel. Like
most writers, I found words dripping with ambrosia at their
birth curled the tongue like vinegar in adolescence. I
reworked the piece until a reading didn't riddle me with
depression or drive me to pull my hair with cries of *you're
no writer,* clacking through my head like a Smith-Corona. In
typical show biz fashion, I connected with the Hollywood
editor through a friend of a friend of a... You get the picture.

At last the 'call', an email in late June. Adrenaline
surged as I clicked on the message. *Come to Hollywood in
July.* Nothing more. No hint, no clue. Did she like the
manuscript or loathe it? Scenarios raced through my mind.

Of course she hated it, she would have said otherwise. No, wait. How could she not marvel at its sheer brilliance? She'd suggest a publisher; recommend a screenwriting collaborator. Perhaps she already forwarded the manuscript, marked with superlatives, to an agent or even a studio.

The day of reckoning arrived. Anxiety gripped me as it had in college when I scanned grade postings outside a professor's door. Agitated with worry and hope, I boarded a plane at O'Hare. Settling into my seat, I inhaled—another leg of the journey behind me—now, just the flight, drive...and feedback. Smooth sailing? The pilot's voice crackled through cabin speakers, *"Ladies and gentlemen, an indicator light... asked mechanics to... might only be... or could be... I'll give an update..."* Minutes ticked across the one-hour mark. A creeping delay threatened my appointment with destiny. Hollywood didn't wait. Great ideas were a dime a dozen. Planes, trains and automobiles arrived daily brimming with those eager for discovery, and left again with the dejected.

But a scurrying huddle of uniforms fixed the plane. Four and a half hours later, we landed in LA. Because of delay, I had only enough time to collect a rental car and drive to the meeting—no coffee, no bathroom break, no opportunity to circle the block to calm last-minute jitters. Armed with GPS, I charted my course. North on La Cienega, the giant, white letters spelling, *Hollywood* guided me. My body told me I neared my destination. A right onto Santa Monica Boulevard—my heart beat faster, stomach churned, and sweaty hands clutched the wheel. Underarms perspired despite arctic blasts directed at them from the vents.

Last turn, a left onto one of the pretty, tree-lined streets that run between Santa Monica and Sunset Boulevards. With Hollywood's hills in front of me, I slowed the car, searching addresses. Houses looked alike—various shades of white stucco, red-tiled roofs and wrought iron trim. Tidy square bungalows from the twenties and thirties with tidy square front gardens. Sprinklers soaked lawns, keeping coarse grass vibrant green. Tiny streams trickled across sidewalks and into the street. The block looked like one I'd seen in an old black and white movie—perhaps a Newsreal of Chaplin's and Pickford's Hollywood. But the images were real—living, breathing color.

The dashboard voice interrupted my focus: *You have reached your destination.* I steered the silver Toyota to the curb, checking and rechecking house numbers. I didn't want to waste nerves by ringing at the wrong house, not to mention embarrassment of doubling back to the right one. What if she were watching? She'd already cast judgment on my work and writing abilities. I didn't want her also to judge me an imbecile.

I cut the engine and pulled my leather satchel from the passenger seat. A lift of the flap confirmed that notebook, pen and manuscript hadn't vanished since my last check— ten minutes before at the stoplight on Wilshire Boulevard.

"This is it," I said, pulling the handle and opening the door. "No turning back."

My bare arms and face embraced the warmth. Sweet aromas of jasmine and gardenia were welcome changes from the blandness of an air-conditioned car. Pulsing sprinkler heads beat a gentle rhythm across the quiet neighborhood. With bag slung over shoulder, I stood and faced the house. While the structure resembled its neighbors, the landscaping didn't. Vines covered cream-colored stucco; untamed shrubbery encroached upon a stone path leading to the house.

As I stood before the entrance, an arched door with an iron-grated window, my stomach soured. I rang the bell and waited, listening for stirrings of my judge, jury and...

The wooden door opened slowly. My eyes traveled from white plaster, down to a pixie of a woman with cropped white hair and twinkling blue eyes. "Welcome. Trust your flight was okay. Just love Chicago." The accent was unmistakably Australian.

She ushered me in. I felt a bit like Gandalf entering a Hobbit's lair. Her home, more cottage than house, brimmed with furnishings and mementos scaled for her impish frame. The room felt warm, cluttered, but comfortable. My eyes did a quick scan—upholstered chairs and sofa trimmed in sherry-hued oak, fringed rugs in shades of brown, red and amber, a cozy fireplace and books everywhere. Large and small volumes of art, architecture and literature spilled from bookshelves onto tables, ottoman and hearth.

With two strides, we were through the living room and into a dining area. She motioned me to a chair at the table. "Tea?"

"Sure," I replied, taking a seat. The table, like everything else was unpretentious, its sheen worn away by time.

She shuffled into the kitchen, partially visible through a wall of shelves filled with knickknacks and vining plants. A ticking mantle clock and twittering of pet birds somewhere beyond my line of sight accompanied the thumping in my chest.

Where to look? Study an aboriginal wood carving on the opposite wall, watch for my host, gaze at a hand-painted fruit bowl on the table? Should I keep hands on my lap, at my side, folded on the table? So much was riding on this meeting, validation that I was on the right track. I had believers back in Chicago, and others who patted my shoulder and said, "Give it a year or two. The corporate world will take you back." But I didn't want to go back. Once I made up my mind, I marched forward. Who had time for rearview mirrors?

With a herald of clanking metal and glass, my host reappeared. As she placed a mug of hot tea and a plate of cookies before me, I studied her? Would her expression and gestures offer a hint? *Did she like my novel*?

She sat at the head of the table, no mug for herself. As we exchanged pleasantries, I felt as if I were on a visit to great aunty's. I poured milk into my tea, and broke an almond cookie in half before nibbling off an end. Familiar aromas swirled from the warm liquid and soothed. No sooner had my heart slowed and breathing calmed, than the small woman with kind smile and crinkled eyes took charge. The last bite of cookie wasn't down my throat before she transformed from pixie to professor, from aunt to antagonist. She offered tea, but no sympathy.

"Open your notebook," she said, tapping table. "Write this down."

I felt as if I'd shrunk. Perhaps, she grew. I lost track of time as editor rattled off my infractions. With my head bent over the table, her words barked into my ears. "Bad font. Twelve point's best, Times New Roman. Always paginate, double space. Never two sided. Never bound. Indent paragraphs." She scoffed at extra spaces I'd inserted between paragraphs. "Where'd you learn that?"

As my pen flew across and down the page, I kept thinking, *B...but did she like my novel?*

An answer came fast and furiously. Pixie vanished, replaced by editor and judge. She produced my manuscript from a pile of papers on the far side of the table. Why hadn't I seen it? Had she purposely kept it camouflaged to avoid distracting me during her pedantic drill? The papers she slid toward her looked worn, dog-eared, disheveled. A far cry from the crisp, creaseless and bleached white bundle I delivered with accomplishment and high hopes and yes, love. Was that how a parent felt collecting a bullied child from school—their spotless little angel, scuffed, battered and scraped by a schoolyard hooligan?

She sighed. "Quite maddening it was. Trying to read...*this*." She held up a page, frayed edges, telltale signs of where she'd torn it from its binding. With a roll of her eyes, she flicked the page over. "Two-sided," she groaned, a look of disdain as if I'd just poured ketchup on Chateaubriand. Here was a teacher who practiced audial and visual reinforcement.

Her reproach stung. "Sorry," was the best I could offer. Sight of my dissected manuscript pained me. *She didn't hate my novel, she loathed it. Probably disliked me as well.* I sipped tea, but gone were any calming properties. Cookies sat abandoned on the plate; my stomach tumbled. I tried to get comfortable, teeter-tottering from butt cheek to butt cheek. My shirt rode up, damp seams pinching my armpits. Despite my disappointment, I mustered strength to appear both concerned by and receptive to her critique. *Feedback is good, a gift that makes us better writers.* The words clacked in my head, as futile as a Band Aid to mend a gaping wound.

"Well," she said, her tone flipping to chipper, "let's start with the good news."

Okay, I thought. *Better. All's not lost. Hang in there.* I perked up, nodding for her to proceed.

"Well, you can write. Your sentences string together, no question about it."

"Oh, that's good." Then I thought some more. How was that good? Hadn't she just complimented me for passing fifth-grade language arts? My mind raced to the classroom of Sister Maria Ann, a nun teased for green hair and feared for flashes of anger. Nun tapped blackboard, instructing us how to diagram a sentence. *Well done, Sister.*

"And you've got a great story," the pixie added.

Not bad. A good story is the heart of a novel.

"I mean it," she added, probably sensing my doubt. "You've got a wonderful villain."

I breathed a sigh of relief. The car wasn't totaled. I could drive away from this hit and run. I braced for the, *but.* It was coming that much I knew. Only question was when.

"Now," she said, pulling down on her white sweater, "you didn't pay me to tell you what's good..." *Sensible.* A dentist only inflicted pain on bad teeth. But at least you left his office with a beautiful smile and lollipop.

She sat back in her chair. "Let me ask you something." My manuscript teetered on her knee. "Have you ever read a novel?"

I gasped. That was like asking a baker if she used an oven, or a chauffeur if he drove a car. "Y..yes. I was an English major. R...read all the time, still do." I stammered, trying to mount a defense.

My credentials didn't faze her. "*This* reads like a docudrama."

Now I understood why she repeatedly referred to my manuscript as *this*. Like that awkward moment when a stranger meets a new mother with an androgynous baby swaddled in yellow or green. She couldn't categorize it. Worse than a homely baby, my beloved creation was a 157,000-word turd pie.

My eyes widened; lips pursed to form a toothless, frozen, and completely fake grin. Pretense was my strength. Lean into the criticism. Ride with her words or buck them, and break. If I acted defensive, I risked looking desperate or worse, foolish.

"I won't go over everything. You can read my notes later."

Oh joy! I nodded for her to proceed.

For the next twenty to thirty minutes, I sat speechless, head nodding as she flipped through the loose sheets scanning for pencil marks. She'd lose a fortune playing poker. When she paused on a page, I braced, cheeks tightening on chair. Forehead creases narrowed; blue eyes lasered on the guilty line. I saw her mind churn, reliving the literary atrocity while trying to find her words.

"Too much. Let the readers think for themselves," she said, after reciting one line. "What's with all the *fucks*? Lose 'em. Oh, oh, here's one," she added with a burst of energy. Had she found a hidden gem? She could hardly contain her joy as she read the sentence. "A real stinker." I laughed too, but slid down in my seat and melted inside. What else could I do, cry? "They have contests for these things, you know...world's worst metaphors. This might win."

Really! Literary contests paved the way for publishing deals. But who draws attention to his own fart? Perhaps she intended to submit it? *Back off, pixie. That may be a stinker, but it's mine*. Copyright laws protected the fair and the foul.

With mounting frustration, I looked for summary judgment and euthanasia. "Should I just dash it all?"

She sat up, her expression hardened. "What? Nonsense. Like I said, it's a great story.

You've got a terrific villain, a real bastard. Americans love to hate CEOs. Fix these things," she added with a tap to the manuscript. "Polish it up. Get it to market fast." *Get it to market?* Of course, every fart dissipates. My manuscript had life—legs, sellable legs. I listened with renewed interest. Sure, she pointed out problems. That's why I paid her. But she also summarized strengths: a solid foundation, believable characters including a compelling hero and villain. I even earned a gold star for knowing my subjects from my predicates.

With coal raking finished, fiendish sprite surrendered to impish pixie. Blue eyes regained their sparkle. Smile returned. "Send me some passages," she said, tidying the paper pile. "Be happy to look them over."

I took that as subtle reassurance, a message not to abandon my dream. Keep trying; keep writing.

She walked me to the cottage door. No agent deal, publishing referral or Hollywood screenplay. Although she offered none of those or even a consolation lollipop, she left me with hope, the fuel that allows writers to face blank pages.

When Hollywood called, it didn't hang up when I answered. The message may not have been the one hoped for, but I had encouragement. Mine was a great story. I just didn't know how to tell it...*yet*.

Nathan Johnson

De Soiree

The event occurred in the north Belgian countryside, in a chateau established more than two hundred years ago. From my earlier experiences in Berlin, I'd learned these European mansions provided accommodations for the upper classes during hunting seasons.

We were inside one of the huge ground floor rooms near the center of the building. Light flickered on a damp stone terrace beyond the glass doors where our dream had earlier begun.

Directly opposite and inside the room was a large fireplace, and tall windows with heavy drapes and thick carved wood paneling.

Previously, over dinner, I was asked by the host what it was in F. Scott Fitzgerald's work "The Great Gatsby" that I found compelling. My reply was "Well, really, it's a story about money. It's that simple really. And that complicated." I recounted how Gatsby's early history as a campaign officer during the war reminded me of a British author I got to know the last time I was in Brussels. His stories of adventure in foreign lands always seemed too incredible to believe, but like Gatsby, when pressed for detail, his stories rang true. From my own time in the US military I could tell—the Brit knew things only those in the Operational world would know.

"Oh, and another thing I'm struck by," I continued, "is the significance of so many celebrated characters at Gatsby's parties, because later when he is so completely and utterly alone his unrequited love for Daisy Buchanan is more painful."

"But," I admitted, "I haven't read it in its entirety."

The host of the party insisted that any guests remaining after midnight would have to join him in acting scenes from stories we'd talked about earlier in the evening.

The nine of us retired to his library. From his insistence, I believe we were expected to have read and thus lived at least some parts of the books up for discussion.

Light from the fireplace and the table illuminated walls stocked with shelves of books.

Our host paused for a moment, and, after scanning the room, located a bound leather case. When he opened it, each book inside had the look of being part of a set, recognizable by the same binding even though they were all of different physical dimension and typeface.

We began with one that had huge nouveau design and lettering on the cover, like a French Farmer's Almanac. It turned out to be a play written by Victor Hugo. As it was being acted, I followed along but felt inadequate, my lack of fluency combined with the drinks I had that night demonstrating a wasted past So I took it upon myself to provide sound effects; a phone ringing, the opening of a door, footsteps. I didn't engage much in the discussion afterward, but listened intently, still interested. But I felt my social status slipping.

The next book introduced I immediately recognized as "The Great Gatsby". I felt as if I'd passed some sort of test because of what I'd said earlier.

The scene we performed was the dinner party where Gatsby encounters golf pro Jordan Baker, and Nick Carraway. What I remembered was that Gatsby, when addressing a man, always seemed to punctuate the end of every sentence with "old sport".

As Gatsby, reading aloud, I didn't have to rely much on the written word to sustain the pace. In the performance, I recognized in myself the desperate protagonist's undeservedly rich, boozy behavior and solitary perspective. It struck me—I was the American—not moneyed, but grasping for social resonance, dulled by alcohol and the likelihood of further isolation soon.

Standing, I noticed that the upper tier of a thick wooden tabletop near us was emitting an array of flames that illuminated only the very center of the room. There was no vent that I could see.

Without pausing, I instinctively put my hand flat out on top of one of the flames.

It immediately went out. I hadn't felt the slightest variation in temperature. I realized that any safety measure would have been a foregone conclusion, the danger engineered out of the equation. One second later I removed my hand, and the flame reappeared. I'm sure my behavior was charming, if only illustrative of a life lived not in Europe, not in first class.

The spirited host began a discussion on each of the literary works we'd read thus far.

I sat, and remained quiet, resisting the urge to be passionate with my opinions, knowing that drinking was hazardous—in more ways than one.

What the hell, I thought. Might as well press forward.

Then I woke up.

David Ellard

meetings

i meet, you meet
every day
on the same street
walking to work
at the same time
but always a day later

i meet, you meet
every day
on the same street
always the same face
but a day older
the girl with the apple round cheeks
scandinavian-style
with the slight unfocused smile

and i wonder
do i look the same to you
and are we two
suspended on a gossamer time thread
while the world around gets younger

i meet, you meet
every day
on the same street

passing, we don't greet

and i wonder
will we ever meet
socially i mean, at a party
and if we do
will it be a meeting of minds
or even bodies
i mate, you mate
it's innate

we'll never know
passing every day
on the same street
at the same time

Essex Goldilocks

So I was goin' down a hill and I woz finkin' like it must be
way past breakfast time an' all tha' and I was ge'ing well
hungry wot wiv wanderin' round in this forest all mornin'
like it's never gonna end an' all tha'. Looks like it's gonna
rain an' all.

I been tryin' to get my mate Sharon on my mobile an'
she's not answerin', I dunno, what she's up to probably
ignorin' me silly cow. Oh yeah there's no like signal innit. In
this forest. Silly me.

No use callin' me mum anyway, she just say: 'I told you
a fousand times, don't go wanderin' off in fairy tale forests
an' all tha'', yeah well I know tha' NOW don' I? Don' exactly
help me now, innit?

So I see this house like at the bo'om of the hill. Well, a bit weird house an all' tha', not like on the estate back in Thanet. So I go down a hill to the house an' start bangin' on the door an' all tha'. "Ere, let me in! I'm starvin' Give us some grub!" But there's no one there an' guess wha'? They left the door open like anyone could walk in and burgle their Sky box innit? Last time we got done in Thanet they nicked me iPod. I ask yer? Ain't no one honest these days?

So I walks in an' it's all weird an' tha' but there's this smell like food comin' from the back an' I walk through into the kitchen it must be an' there's this table wiv three bowls. Looks like somein' well-mingin' in the bowls. Wha' I need is some chips wiv ketchup but instead they've got this like porridge stuff innit?

Still I'm starvin' like I said, so I tries the first bowl, there's this spoon stuck in it, but blimey! almost burns me mouth off. So I tries the next one but it's cold. Urrrgghh! I'm still like starvin' so I tries the third one an' actually it's not bad. So I eat it. Not as good as chips wiv ketchup I like that Heinz stuff be'er than the Cash 'n' Carry ketchup where me mum goes cheap cow.

So I go back in the front room lookin' for the TV coz it's like Hollyoaks on Sky 5 at 9:30 but, can you believe it? There's no telly, like I really fink they must have just got burgled well it's their own fault leavin' the door unlocked. My mate Tracey her older bruvver Terry he done over a warehouse. Got me a new iPod only a tenner. Well good. Be'er than the old one.

There's no telly but I'm feelin' like well sleepy after all that porridge sort of fills you up dunnit? So I fancy havin' a sit-down. There's three chairs, so I try the first one but it's too 'ard innit? The second one's got this like big cushion but

I'm like sinkin' into it worse than that fing in Becky's bedroom, a pouff or some'in she calls it.

But the third one's like nice so I sit on it but, lordy lordy! There's this crack! Next fing I'm on the floor, dunno what I woz doin' like I passed away or some'in. Passed away is it? Na, that's what happened to me Gran Norma in April. Cancer. Passed out that's it. Anyway so I wake up on the floor and there's this chair all broken like.

So I'm finkin like, maybe I should scarper, they might give me one of them ASBOs for like breakin' and entrin' innit? My mate Keira she got one for like spittin' at this old cow who lives down a street from her.

But then I'm still like feelin' well knackered an' that so I fink, upstairs, there must be a bedroom somewhere in this dump innit? I mean no telly, crap chairs innit? So up I go.

Waiting for the Wine

David Ellard reports on an unexpected peril of expatriate life in Brussels

I take the number 20 bus to work in the mornings. From *St. Gilles* along *Rue Blaes* into the old town of Brussels and then up the hill to where the posh people live and out again the other side towards the collection of brutalist structures they call the European District.

Belgians of an older, less cautious generation will tell you that *St. Gilles* has too many Arabs, but I like it. My local, *l'Union*, is full of loafing students and aging anarchists. There's a sign above the door saying *pas de drogue*. I assume it's a good place to buy them.

However there is a price to escaping from the EU ghetto and its bright-eyed students on five-month internships and graveyard weekend *ambience*.

I have to commute to work. You'll see me there at the bus stop outside *Porte de Hal* every weekday morning. If you do, you may even be tempted to ask me directions. Belgians are.

This is a shame for at least two reasons.

Firstly, and sincerely, I really have no idea. I have no sense of direction. It's a source of wonder to me that I managed to steer myself out of my mother's womb down the birth canal and out into the world without wandering into, say, the kidneys or gall bladder *en route*. I assume that was mostly my mother's doing.

I try to be helpful, but I really have no idea. The backpacking guidebooks to India warn you that, if you ask them, locals there will give you random directions to make you feel happy. I like to think that Indian tourists in Brussels consulting me will feel right at home.

Also, I don't have a car. Motorists sometimes stop me, and occasionally I even know where they are now, where they want to go *and* how to get between these two points. But then I invariably steer them the wrong way down a procession of one way streets. 'Ghostdriving', as they call it in Flemish, and I just hope the cops don't get them for it.

Secondly, and even more sincerely, mornings are not my time of day. It's that stretch of time between tumbling out of bed bleary-eyed and reaching the drinks machine in the office that I call Before Coffee. It's a bit like the Before Christ they taught us about at school but a lot longer ago.

I could have coffee at home before I leave I guess, but that would just waste precious seconds of additional sleep time. I need my sleep you see. When that alarm clock blasts on, I am primeval. It's not so much Before Christ as the Dawn of Life on Earth. I lie amoeboid.

I've been living in Brussels for coming up to a decade now and I've noticed a couple of things about the French language. Firstly, they count a bit funny. We say 'eighty' which means eight tens. They say *quatre-vingts* which is four twenties. I guess the Ancient Gauls had twenty fingers each. They've been losing them ever since. It's only a theory, mind.

Secondly, the root of the words for dog (*chien*) and 'to crap' (*chier*) is the same. I think this is some kind of linguistic foreshadowing of the problem of pavement dog turds that so plagues French-speaking cities.

I know quite a few bilingual people here and I sometimes wonder which language they dream in. Does it go by alternate nights, for example?

After almost a decade in Brussels, however, I know I am still at heart English speaking. When I get out of bed in the morning, drag my undead body across to the bathroom and in my stupor stub my big toe against the laundry basket I do not exclaim *Merde!* or even *Godverdomme!*

No, I say *Fuck!* instead. It's all I can manage at this time. One of these days I suspect I will wake up robbed of the power of speech entirely.

My faculties come back gradually during the day, especially After Coffee. By midday I am normally capable of a bright and happy conversation - in French - with my secretary, about her farmhouse in Sardinia say, or post-Hegelian dialectics.

OK maybe not the post-Hegelian dialectics. But Before Coffee, when even my English is severely impaired, it's tricky.

Belgian people like to ask me directions. I think it's because I look unthreatening. I am not tall and, I guess, vaguely pleasant looking. More vague than pleasant in the mornings but *quand même*. Also, I'm wearing a suit and tie and I think that helps. Young mothers wheeling prams can stop and ask me without worrying if I will molest their charges.

It's just such a crying shame really.

The other morning, standing in line as usual for the number 20 bus, someone came up to me and asked perfectly politely: *Monsieur, où est le vin?*

I thought about this for a bit, inasmuch as I could Before Coffee, and replied carefully: *Le vin blanc ou le vin rouge*?

The woman gave me a look that said 'who is this incredibly strange person?' and walked away hurriedly.

It's a crying shame and I'm here to warn you. If you need to know something and you see that well-dressed vaguely pleasant looking moron standing in the bus queue in front of you, please don't ask. I'm busy waiting for the wine.

Martin R. Jones

Dust

Leo Blake sat at his usual table outside The Franklin. It was the first sunny day of spring and people seeking lunch strolled up and down the pavements along rue Archimède chattering cheerfully in a dozen languages; most of which he didn't understand. From his seat he could see the arms of the Berlaymont reaching out towards him. He glanced across at his companion. He's starting to look his age, he thought.

'Another drink, Jacob?'

'Why not?'

He beckoned towards the waitress. 'Deux bières, s'il vous plaît.'

They sat silently. What was there to say? All their conversation was used up. He suddenly felt tired. Sixty-five is a dangerous age. It was the age when you had most to say, but when no-one listens. Your body starts playing tricks on you. The digestion is not what it was, thinning hair is little more than a wistful memory and a bout of indigestion rouses fears of a heart-attack. He regarded Rasmussen sourly. And all your friends resemble you. No escape there.

'Shall we join the others inside?'

Rasmussen seemed relieved. 'Yes, let's.'

Lounging against the bar were the usual crowd. He could tell by their red faces that they had already been drinking heavily. McMasters was at the fag-end of a joke and they all laughed dutifully. Except for Andersson, who smiled doubtfully, as if unsure he had understood. To cover his uncertainty he leant down to scratch the ears of his dog, which sat at his feet with an air of forlorn patience. It was a scruffy little thing, and greying at the muzzle. Andersson had once told Blake it was a Swedish breed. A Vallhund, or something like that. He had said it reminded him of home.

'Decided to be sociable, have you,' said McMaster challengingly. He was one of those aggressively gregarious types who regard a lack of conviviality as a direct slight. He came from Edinburgh, though you wouldn't know by his accent.

Blake didn't reply.

'I was just telling the others that my daughter is coming over for a few days,' said Warnock. 'Haven't seen her for a couple of years. She moved back to Britain, you know.'

'Yes, we did,' sighed Kilgallen wearily. He wore round, dark-rimmed glasses, a moustache balanced above his thin mouth. Sometimes he sported a fedora, tilted back on his head. Aping James Joyce Blake had always sneeringly assumed. He drained his glass and signalled for another. While he waited his eyes roved the bar. Sitting at a table by the window were a young couple, a *pichet* of house white between them. The man looked ill-at-ease, by his slightly scruffy clothes he didn't work in one of the nearby offices. The girl had the look of a stagiare; fresh-faced and expensively dressed. She had one of those clear home counties voices and it cut through the buzz of conversation in the bar.

'My boss says he thinks I have real talent. He wants me to write a follow-up report. Of course, it means I'll have to stay on.'

Her companion appeared a little distraught. He refilled their glasses.

'Of course,' he said.

'If I do a good job it might mean we can move here permanently.'

Blake felt a surge of envy. She was no more than twenty. She still had choices.

'But what about my job?' asked the man.

'Oh, I'll be able to support you,' she said blithely. 'Do you know what Angelopoulos said?'

'Who's Angelopoulos?'

'The MEP. Don't you ever listen? Of course, I'll have to join a party,' she went on. 'It's an advantage to be political. Which one do you think would be best?'

'I'm sure I don't know.'

The girl's glance roamed around the room disinterestedly. Her eye fell on Blake, but she gave no sign of registering him, of even noting his existence. He wanted to say to her: "Are you certain that's what you want? Look around you. Do you want to end up like us, people with nothing to do and with nowhere to go?"

'Anyway, I'm not sure I want to live here. I like it where I am.'

'Well, I don't,' she said harshly. 'You know, I don't think that you want to stay with me, do you?'

'Of course I do. It's just....'

At that point Warnock asked him if he wanted another drink so Blake never discovered what 'it's just' was. When he looked back the man was examining the bill. He reached for his wallet.

'No, I'll pay,' the girl said loftily. 'It's my celebration.'

The man shrugged hopelessly. Blake had thought they were a well-matched pair. Now he could see they weren't. They reached for their coats and left, the girl leading the way.

Blake turned his attention back to his friends. Warnock was saying,' You know, I've had enough here. I'm thinking of buying a place in Sussex.'

Blake looked at him with contempt. No you won't, he thought. There's nothing there for you. You don't know anyone. You'll just get older and feebler and then they'll sell your house to pay for a nursing home.

'Galways's nice,' cut in Kilgallen wistfully. 'It's where my mother's family come from.' He drained his beer and ran a hand over his moustache. 'But my wife says she couldn't stand being in Ireland. She wants to go back to Germany. Germany's alright, but I don't want to live there. I suppose we'll just stay.'

'Oh, one place is much like another,' said Rasmussen, 'after you've been there a while.'

The crowd in the bar started to thin as the customers began to drift back to work. Blake glanced up at the clock behind the bar. It was only half past two. He had all the time in the world. He signalled to the barmaid for another drink.

'Anyone care to join me?'

'Not for me,' mumbled Andersson, patting his stomach. 'Doctor's orders.'

'Getting old, are we?' said McMaster, maliciously. He'd always despised Andersson.

'I'd better go too,' said Rasmussen. 'My wife wants me to pick up some things from the supermarket.'

'Well, you'd better go then, hadn't you?' McMasters tone was dismissive, bitter. Almost in spite of himself Blake felt a lurch of compassion. McMaster's wife had died some time ago. He had no-one to go home to.

Rasmussen eyed McMaster sourly. He turned to Andersson. 'Come on. Let's go.'

He made for the door. Andersson hurried after him, shoulders hunched. His dog struggled to its feet and followed. The door slammed behind them.

McMaster made a dismissive grunt. Blake could see he was quite drunk.

They drank their beer morosely.

'Fancy a change of scene?' asked Warnock.

'Why not,' said Kilgallen.

'I'm staying put,' slurred McMasters. He was leaning heavily against the bar, his eyes bloodshot.

'Suit yourself,' said Kilgallen. He glanced towards Blake. 'Coming, Leo?'

'Alright,' said Blake. 'See you tomorrow John,' he said to McMasters. He didn't reply, turning his back and hunching over the bar. Blake shrugged and followed the others. They waited for a gap in the stream of grey cars and crossed the road to Le Faubourg. Although it was still too early for the office crowd, stopping for a drink on their way home, the bar was bustling. A radio behind the bar leaked a faint stream of Europop. Sitting by the door were a group of tourists; Chinese? Japanese? Blake could never tell. They were jabbering excitedly and taking photographs of each other with their telephones. The woman who always reminded Blake of Degas; 'Absinthe' was at her usual table, sitting upright and unseeing, a glass of red wine in front of her.

They ordered three Stellas and found a table by the window. Warnock and Kilgallen fell into a half- hearted argument about the relative merits of Galway and Sussex; the price of property, the quality of the pubs. Blake let his mind drift, back to his last day at work. Was it only six months ago? His boss had made a speech referring to his dedication to the job, throwing in a couple of amusing anecdotes for good measure. His colleagues had wished him luck and urged him to enjoy his well-earned leisure. They had given him an expensive watch in a presentation case. Why do they give you a watch when you retire? For all those urgent appointments you can't afford to miss? He smiled sourly. He was not a sentimentalist, he told himself. He knew that no-one would regret him going and in a few months he would be forgotten. Then his wife had left. She said he was cluttering up the house, she needed space to 'grow'. As a parting shot, she had told him that she'd never really loved him anyway. Well, that explained a lot. Resurfacing, he heard Warnock telling Kilgallen brightly that, Yes, he thought he might well contact some estate agents, pop over to England for a few days, see what was available. Kilgallen replied enthusiastically, and yes, he might talk to his wife tonight. She might be persuaded.

He surveyed them bitterly, with their drink-fuelled optimism. He wondered at human beings capacity for self-deception; their pitiable and baseless optimism.

Then he heard Warnock say 'I ought to be going, before the Metro gets too crowded.'

'Me too,' said Kilgallen

'Not just yet,' said Blake.

'See you tomorrow then,' said Warnock.

Kilgallen peered at him through his glasses. 'Same time, same place.'

He suddenly felt lonely.

They waved cheerily as they left. At that moment he hated them for all their hopeless dreams.

*

As he walked home the sun was beginning to set, his shadow preceded him up Avenue Charlemagne. Some lines from *The Wasteland* rose unbidden, and he mouthed them silently.

'Your shadow at evening rising to meet you.

I will show you fear in a handful of dust.'

Christ, that's a bleak thought he said to himself, with a grim bravado which, in his heart of hearts, he knew he didn't feel. Then he was gripped by a sudden panic. He was pretty certain that there was no whiskey in the house. Luckily, with a sense of relief, he noticed an *épicerie*. He pushed his way through the door and it softly clicked shut behind him.

Klavs Skovsholm

Paper Angel

Late one Christmas Eve, Robert the Rat did what he did so well: nimbly trotting along on the edge of the gutter. Testing himself, he moved as quickly as he could, placing his small paws in a thin line right on the very edge. He liked to push himself to prove that he could still move as swiftly as his numerous younger nieces and nephews. Too many names for him to remember, his brothers and sisters had simply been too prolific breeders. While not shying away from the occasional piece of tail, Robert had preferred to stay a bachelor, never having cared for commitments. However, this evening he had felt very lonely without any family of his own. "A power walk will do me good," he had thought.

As he came power walking along, his eye briefly caught sight of a paper angel drifting aimlessly and abandoned in the icy current of water caused by the recent rainfall. It had glittered briefly in the headlights of a passing car. He stopped. Then Robert backtracked to where the angel was slowly moving towards the drain further down the road. He observed her and, as she turned in the current, he saw her pleading eyes before her head with a golden crown plunged back into the water. His first inclination was to leave her to her own devices. Then he changed his mind. After all, it was Christmas Eve.

He quickly moved forward to where the gutter stones were lower and overflowing with water. There he stretched out and grabbed a wing tip by his teeth. He pulled the paper angel out of the water with ease and sat her down on the pavement before resuming his trot along the gutter. Nothing pleased Robert the Rat better than strutting his stuff.

He felt proud of his balancing act and wished someone had been around to see him. He was so full of himself that it took a moment before he noticed that an on-coming car swayed dangerously and hit a puddle of water sending a wave of rainwater his way. "Must be a drunk driver," Robert thought and he agilely jumped aside. As he turned to follow the car with his eyes, he saw that the wave had washed the paper angel into the gutter.

Although not prone to being sentimental (what's sentimental about a rat's life after all?) he dived into the current. The drain was about to expedite the paper angel into the watery underworld of the city. The water was picking up speed, but Robert had no difficulty in rescuing the paper angel. He was as fit as a fiddle and an excellent swimmer by nature. A few moments later, they found themselves on the pavement. They were soaked, but unharmed.

Robert now looked at the paper angel and wondered what had been the sense of his rescuing her? All wet for a piece of glittering paper! He always looked out for himself and he expected something in return for favors. If the angel had been clumsy enough to get herself into trouble by falling into the gutter, she should have been smart enough to get herself out of trouble, too. Still, instead of walking away, he sat down and watched as the paper angel started to dry. He wondered if she had drowned? Her eyes were closed and she was all pale. Surprisingly, the frosty air quickly dried the dress which turned into a vivid and sparkling white and gold before his eyes. Now, she had bright red cheeks. Suddenly she opened her eyes and broke into a smile. She seemed to glow a little in the dark.

"I shall be indebted to thee for ever and ever after. Thou hast saved my life at the risk of thy own!" the angel said gratefully.

"Don't mention it", Robert answered, shrugging his shoulders, as he wondered why she spoke like in the old tales his mother had told him and his many siblings as bedtime stories. He felt noble at heart.

"I shall reward thee!" the angel said.

The mentioning of a reward made Robert prick up his ears.

"Reward? What kind of reward?" he asked, his heart now overflowing with curiosity and ratty self-interest.

"Thou must help me first," the paper angel countered, sensing his change of heart.

"How?" Robert felt slightly peeved that rescuing her from the icy current of water did not in itself entitle him to some reward.

"I slipped from the loving fingers of a child intent on placing me on top of a Christmas tree. The child's name is Peter and he is now greatly upset. He wanted to present me as a gift to his ailing grandmother. Help me find that tree so Peter will be happy again."

The angel sent Robert a questioning glance. Robert was unmoved by this talk about an upset boy named Peter and his sick grandmother.

"Thou reward will be more than thou can dream of," the angel said raising her voice.

Although a bit weary of possible dangers (a wise rat should never disregard these!) the promise of an unimaginable reward was too tempting, so he accepted to help.

Robert left with the paper angel on his back in search of Peter. They searched many a deserted street. On and on they pressed. Robert thought it must be midnight soon.

Whizzing along at a good speed, and the paper angel holding on for dear life, Robert suddenly stopped in his tracks propelling the lovely creature on his back to fly forward head first. He knew he should help her up, but his mind was foremost on their safety. The moonlight was lighting up several pairs of eyes hiding in the shadows behind a garbage can. He knew that kind of reflection all too well: Cats eyes!

Robert quickly scanned his surroundings for a way out of trouble: No drains close by they could dive into; solid house walls without drainpipes and open road. Only a single parked car offered a vantage point.

"Cunning bastards, those cats!" he swore.

He seriously considered abandoning the paper angel to save his own skin. Then he thought better of it and decided they were in this together.

The paper angel had managed to get up by her own means and was dusting dirt of her dress when she felt Robert grab tightly on to her wings and drag her off brusquely. He made for the car. She realized their predicament as she saw four alley cats emerge out of the dark, slowly moving towards them.

Robert knew from experience that cars were harder to climb than houses. Yet, he was confident that he could gain them a moment of safety. A few moments later they were on the roof of the car. He quickly glanced at the paper angel to see if any help was at hand, but she was stiff with fright.

The cats had now taken up position on the car: two on the bonnet and the other two on the boot. Robert felt trapped. The cats enjoyed the spectacle of their prey being consumed by fear before they would eat them alive. Robert only knew too well how chillingly sadistic cats are.

"I can help," cried the angel mustering some courage. "Throw me into the air so I can spread some magic angel dust. That'll scare them!"

Robert kept his eyes on the cats while all his muscles tensed up.

The monsters were now readying themselves to jump onto the car's roof, but they nervously hesitated because of an approaching taxi. It approached slowly checking house numbers with a search light. Robert saw his chance! Rather attempt the near impossible than being painfully killed by cats.

"No time for angel dust!" he yelled.

Holding on to the angel, he took a couple of paces back. Then he speeded towards the edge of the car's roof and, with all his might, he jumped into the void between him and the approaching taxi. Miraculously, he landed on the roof of the taxi. He held on the best he could, his small claws hurting and making scratching noises on the hard surface. As the car turned the corner, he made out the outraged cats on the parked car. His heart pounded wildly and he was sweating profusely. He was relieved, too. Then he grinned with satisfaction. "If only my nieces and nephews could see me now," he thought. The paper angel was petrified.

A few streets away, the vehicle stopped to let its passengers out. Robert decided it was time to get off discreetly. He did not want to be seen. He knew how irrational some humans react at the sight of the likes of him and he was in no need of extra commotion.

The paper angel pointed at the house on the opposite side of the street. That house was dark and uninviting.

"This is it! Get us inside."

"Shouldn't be difficult," answered Robert confidently.

"Don't underestimate thy task."

Robert looked around. Neither cats, nor dogs or humans were in sight. He looked up at the door. It had a mail slot, but he was not sure if he could squeeze through. Then he noticed the Beware Dog-sign on the door. He did not like the sight of it, but he could think of no other way in. He gently picked up the angel and readied himself before jumping for the mail slot in the door. The angel closed her eyes in fear. Robert barely managed to heave themselves up and squeeze through the slot.

Soon they were on the floor in the entry hall. All seemed clear. Robert sniffed the air. No trance of any dog smell. "The sign must be a hoax," he realized. He had to sit a moment to catch his breath. His body was shaking.

"Piece of cake," Robert lied as he let go of the angel who fell over on the floor.

"Alright love?" he asked.

"Yes. I think I can still flap my wings." She got up with difficulty.

"Go ahead, then. Flap them!"

"A simple rat like thee, shall not tell me, a paper angel, when to flap my wings or not!" For an instant the glow around her turned an angry red so he said no more. The angel turned white and smiled again.

"Inside these walls, we will find Peter's Christmas tree."

They continued their search. A door was ajar leading from the hall into another room. The moment they had crossed the threshold into the next room, the angel made a sign for Robert to stop. He sat the angel down on the floor. They listened. Dead quiet. There was something eerie about this room.

Suddenly, the door closed behind them with a big bang. Robert jumped up and the hair rose on his back. A big clock began to chime. He counted the strokes. It was midnight.

Outside the clouds were shifting, allowing the silvery moonlight to pour through the windows and reflect on the surface of the floor. The embers in the fireplace woke up and broke out into small bright flames. Their reflections were dancing on the floor.

Right in the middle of the room was a Christmas tree! Only the lower part was clearly visible in the light of the flames. The bright ornaments on its branches were glittering. In his long rat life, Robert had never seen anything so beautiful. His eyes filled with tears and he held a paw to his heart. Leaving the angel behind, he walked up to the tree. He looked at the parcels. They were like massive boulders between him and the tree. He would have to climb to get to it. Several of the parcels had small notes tied to them with the name Peter written on them.

Then he heard commotion coming from behind the tree. Jumping up onto the parcels, he climbed forward to scout over the edge of one of them to see what was going on. He saw four mice beating up an outnumbered pink teddy bear. The poor creature groaned and frantically fought back with her soft fluffy limbs. As all rats, Robert detested mice, but loved a merry fight so he jumped into the midst of the mice throwing himself at them. The mice were small, but tough, and Robert had to bite, scratch and whip with his tail to drive them back. Blood was dripping from his tail when they finally fled.

Robert wanted to lie down to rest, but the pink teddy bear drowned him in fluffy hugs, kissing him repeatedly. With her sugar sweet voice she praised his heroic efforts so profusely that he felt embarrassed. Then they heard the angel cry out. Sprinting as fast as they could, they saw several mice pulling maliciously at the angel's wings. The pink teddy bear ran upright towards two of the mice and she bounced them away with her big belly while Robert bit and scratched the other mice as hard as he could. The mice ran away and Robert and the teddy bear collapsed on the floor.

"Quick," said the paper angel in a weak voice. "Help me up somewhere high so I can get to fly and spread some angel dust. That way I can save us!"

"From what?"

"From the mice. They will be back in the thousands in no time."

The paper angel gave Robert a commanding look. The pink teddy bear started whining. She tried to hide under some of the parcels.

"Just listen!" The paper angel was right. From far away, they heard the sound of hundreds and hundreds of running mice. The noise was increasing fast as the creatures were approaching. Now even Robert got scared. The pink teddy bear was hysterically trying to climb on to the top of the parcels. She kept falling down.

Picking up the paper angel, Robert jumped and landed on the top of the pile of parcels. He reached for the stem of the tree and started climbing with the angel on his back. They were both scratched in the process.

"Hurry up!" the angel commanded.

Within seconds, Robert was well up into the tree and hastily started to crawl towards the end of a branch. It swayed dangerously under him. He almost lost his grip before releasing the paper angel into the air.

Then he saw the mice coming! They came in their hundreds, running towards the tree. They were like soldiers spreading out on a battlefield. The angel tumbled down, flapping her wings ineffectively while spreading angel dust in her fall. The angel dust fell onto the floor spreading out like glittering fog. At first, the mice were undeterred. A few let themselves be engulfed by the fog. Suddenly, out of the fog, a giant shining cobra rose, striking left and right. It sent all the mice scrambling for their lives.

"I knew it!" Robert thought as he looked on." Mice are such cowards!"

A few moments later the dust had dissipated. Calm reigned in the house again. The clock chimed and it struck one.

Back on the floor, Robert looked up at the paper angel who was stuck on a branch. She was lifeless now. Her red cheeks and glow were gone. The pink teddy bear, too, was but a teddy bear again.

"What now?" he thought. He glanced back at the paper angel with disappointment. He felt conned. Stupidly he had believed the angel's promise of a reward. "Is this all I got out of my curiosity? Of my bravery?" he thought. Still, he felt happy that he had been able to help the paper angel. His heart was no longer overflowing with ratty self-interest.

Then he walked a few paces and sat down on the floor, drawing his bleeding tail unto him, holding it tightly while swaying a little to and fro for comfort. His mother had always held him tightly, rocking him, when he had felt distressed.

He was about to look for a way out when he saw a stray parcel note with the name of Peter on it. He grinned, picked it up and tied it around the neck of the pink teddy bear.

"There's a surprise for you, Peter!"

Then he realized that he had one more thing to do. He climbed back up the tree and dislodged the paper angel from the branch where she was stuck. Carefully, he continued his climb and gently placed her on the top of the tree.

Back on the floor, he sat down and looked up towards the angel. Suddenly he heard a faint noise behind him. He looked around and noticed that, at the other end of the room, the double doors were opening graciously like giant white wings. In the adjacent room a table filled with every delight of Christmas was waiting for him. Robert started to weep in gratitude.

He heard the angel's whisper: "This is thy reward. Merry Christmas!"

More Than Meets The Eye

Philip was deeply concentrated in his attempt to hack a homophobic website. He hated these websites. They had been mushrooming on the internet under the lax regulations put in place by the new, right-wing government. He knew it was against the law what he was doing. However, he did something good by shutting down a few of these sites spreading their propaganda of intolerance. A pearl of sweat detached itself from the rim of Philip's blond curly hair. It ran down his temple and over his delicate cheek bones. The computer screens reflected in his reading glasses. He withdrew his slender hands from the keyboard. He took a deep breath. Then he pressed enter and he pushed his chair a little back from his work station. All he could do now was to wait: allow the machine time to search a way past the other computer's firewall.

His phone rang. He was unhappy about the interruption, but when he saw the name of his old friend Bill on the display he picked up the phone anyway. He checked his watch. It was 9.30 pm.

"Hello," he answered irritated.

"Hello, my dearest IT queen!" Bill sounded tipsy.

"Is that what you call me at home, Bill?"

"Of course, not darling. Winerthur does!" He laughed. Philip could hear that he had to be in some café or pub. He frowned. Bill was never going to change.

"I'm down at *Siegfried and Joel*. Come down! I've got something I *must* talk to you about!" Bill said.

"You know what time it is?"

"Never mind! It's only a five minute walk. Do come over, I'll have them put a bottle of bobbles in a cooler while I'm waiting for you."

At that moment his computer indicated that a virus had successfully been installed. "Bingo," he thought. "Now someone just needs to open that e-mail and they're in deep shit." With a smile on his face, he drew his attention back to Bill.

"Alright then! Let me just get my jacket and shoes on. I feel in a festive mood all of a sudden!"

In the hall he briefly stopped to look himself up and down in the mirror. He saw the reflection of his own slim body. He had a difficult time in loving himself. He was slender and feminine. He would have loved to be different, larger and more masculine. His appearance had already caused him so much bullying and pain. As he made for the door, he pushed his depressive mood away, reminding himself of the fact that there were very few things that he could not do.

*

During daytime *Siegfried and Joel's* main draw was their fabulous chocolate cake, but at night it was more a place for an intimate glass of champagne or a cocktail. The café had gained a lot of popularity with a crowd of discerning younger men who appreciated the sophistication of the place. The service was provided by equally hand-picked waiters. Interestingly, the most recent owners of *Siegfried and Joel* had decided to keep its original interior, which was a bit of *belle époque* thrown in with something like a Vienna coffee shop. Very stylish, but very different to the otherwise popular lounge bars in the center of town.

While waiting for Philip to turn up, Bill nipped at a glass of champagne from the cooling bottle. He had had several cocktails already. Through the large windows he had a splendid view. The Opera house was located on the opposite side of the square. A pompous equestrian statue in the middle dominated it. Bill loved the sight of the Opera house: its old massive stairs leading up from the street, flanked by statues and lamps. That building had seen the beginning of many a festive evening and early hours of the morning, late night visits to restaurants, bars and brothels. And not to forget: this was where he had met Winerthur during the intermission of the opera *Masquerade* some years earlier.

A few minutes later Philip walked through the rotating door. He took in the room before he headed for Bill's table and elegantly sat down.

"So, Bill, what brings you to town this time of the day?"

Bill smirked and looked deliberately coy.

"Winerthur just left for London to attend some business. I come straight from the airport," he said.

He lit a cigarette and leaned back in his comfortable chair with a look of satisfaction on his face. Had it not been for his charismatic personality Bill would have looked very average with his straight brown hair and non-descript features. Bill knew that so he compensated by always dressing well and bestowing his cheerful personality on any person he met.

"When the cat's away, the mice will play," Phillip said teasingly.

"Yes, something like that," Bill replied up-beat. He took a puff of his cigarette.

"No, it's not at all that bad. He is a really nice person and I love him, but being a *hausfrau* to a middle aged man is difficult sometimes."

Philip looked at him attentively, curious about what else his friend would tell him.

"You know, Philip, it can be taxing to always have to behave correctly. He is overly concerned about his reputation. Well, I really shouldn't complain. He gives me everything and asks very little in return. Still, I am in limbo between being a lover and a housekeeper.

"Does he mind you seeing other guys?"

"He's very relaxed about it. As long as I don't do it right in front of him and take care of the domestic situation. I always play it safe, of course."

Bill put out his cigarette, but he immediately changed his mind and lit up another one.

"Anyway, Phillip" he said. "It wasn't Winerthur I wanted to talk to you about."

"What then?"

"Well, I need a little help, or rather Mark does."

"Mark? The fashion designer?"

"Yes. Exactly. You know this time of the year he's presenting his new collection."

"And what does that have to do with me? Does he need a new website?" Phillip asked surprised.

"Oh, that's simple," Bill said and paused briefly while puffing at his cigarette. "He's got this great idea of a presentation at the *Naughty Duckling* – by drag queens. So he wondered if you might be able to help?"

"I'm not a drag queen as far as I know," Phillip answered irritably. He hated to be reminded that he looked feminine.

Bill leaned forward with pleading eyes. He had obviously made a promise he was now worried he might not be able to keep.

"Maybe not, sweetie. But you are so good at it."

"When I was a teenager, Bill. Ages ago."

"You still look fabulous! And you know, my love, there are things in life one doesn't forget how to do." Bill squeezed Phillip's hand and sent him another loving glance.

Philip looked wearily at Bill.

"Please Philip. Do say yes. Please!"

"The *Naughty Duckling* – what can I say. It's chic, that's for sure." He smiled faintly.

"So can I tell Mark that you're willing to help him?" Bill asked happily.

"Let me have a look at the dresses first. No promises." Philip moved uneasy in his chair.

"I love you!" Bill laughed heartily and hugged Philip across the table. After a few moments Philip relaxed and hugged him back, laughing, too.

*

"Would you like me to bring you to something? Like a few cuckoo clocks?" Winerthur teased as he turned towards Bill and Philip. He stood in the doorway of the high-speed train to Munich. Winerthur was always travelling for business.

"By all means! What's a home without a cuckoo clock?" Philip replied.

"Quite right! And do keep an eye on Bill for me, won't you? So he doesn't get into trouble." Winerthur smiled and winked at Bill, who pretended to be upset at his lover's last remark.

"I'll get my dog to watch him." Bill laughed.

The train conductor passed by and asked passengers to step back from the automatic doors. Bill quickly ducked forward and kissed his lover as the doors were closing.

Bill and Philip stayed by the tracks until the train had left the station. Freezing autumn wind was sweeping across the platforms. They were glad to get out of the cold as they took the escalators to the upper level of the building.

While leisurely crossing the large hall, Bill stopped at a kiosk to buy some cigarettes and a chocolate bar. A few shops had already started to decorate their showcases for Christmas.

"Maybe we should take the side exit," Bill suddenly said as they approached a small group of people. Philip, who had been admiring some posters, looked ahead and saw what had caused Bill's remark. A couple of young men in the unmistakable uniform of the right wing party were busy enlisting people. They were handing out folders and forms. One man in particular made Philip shiver. It was a guy with a shaven head who had an especially bullying way of addressing people who were passing by. His face had a frightening coldness to it.

They stood still and observed.

"They are disgusting," Bill said. "Come, let's go." He bit firmly into the chocolate bar.

Philip felt anger surface. He had never seen the man before, but he knew that it was his sort that would engage in gay bashing and spreading propaganda of intolerance.

"We've got to do something, Bill," he said.

"There's nothing we can do."

"There must be something..." Philip replied, looking around.

"Isn't your illegal hacking of websites, enough?" Bill whispered with a desperate edge to his voice. "You know how seriously the new government looks at these things."

"Tell you what: Hurry and get the car out in front of the main entrance!"

"But I am not allowed to park there." Bill whined, as he noticed the angry look on his friend's face.

"Bill, just do it! Okay!?"

Bill did as he was told. He ran to his car to bring it up to the front entrance.

In the meantime, Philip looked for an opportunity of some sort. Then he saw it coming: An elderly man, wearing a coat and a hat, was slowly walking in the direction of the crowd of people. He carried a solid umbrella over his arm. Philip quickly got himself in position to walk behind the man. Starring at the guy with the shaven head, he caught his eye as he calmly proceeded. The man stopped what he was doing. An air of evil delight swept over his face. At this point, Philip grabbed the umbrella and swiftly placed a blow over the face of the young man. And then he ran. The other guy cried out in pain. But no one managed to react before the attacker had reached the exit.

Bill gunned the car as soon as Philip was in the passenger seat.

"What did you do?" he asked nervously as he turned the corner and was out of sight.

"I blew someone a blow."

"What?! How could you? Why?"

"How could I not?"

Bill looked at Philip, who met his eye. Philip's hands started to shiver now that he was able to relax. He would never have thought that he would attack anyone. It dawned on him that the authorities would now look at him as a criminal in more than one respect.

"Well, you're absolutely right," Bill said.

"Yeeha!" Bill yelled as he pushed the accelerator down, just making it across an intersection before the lights turned red. He headed towards home: the ochre yellow house where he had always felt so safe. On route, they stopped to buy food so they could have dinner together.

*

"Off to the kitchen," Philip laughed as he entered the hall carrying a couple of bags full of foodstuff. Bill followed with a white cyclamen in each hand.

The kitchen was hidden away in the large old house and equipped to cater for large dinner parties.

"They are really beautiful these cyclamen," Bill said. "I've always liked cyclamen. Winerthur says that they remind him of his brother."

"How come?"

"Ah yes, his brother is a bit of a plant freak. He has a large greenhouse full of them. He can talk about them for hours, if you'd let him. There are many varieties, did you know?"

"I had no idea." Philip answered amused.

Bill got a bottle out of the fridge and two glasses from one of the cupboards. He poured some wine into the glasses before proposing a small toast. Then, he placed their dinner in the microwave oven.

"There's something I want to tell you, Philip." Suddenly he turned very serious.

Philip nodded slightly in anticipation of what was to follow.

"Winerthur has pretty much decided to move abroad as soon as he can rent out the house."

Philip hesitantly put his glass down on the kitchen counter.

"But why?"

"He's worried … he doesn't feel safe. Worried about the direction the country has taken. You've seen what's going on: the new government… the religious extremists…"

He knew that Winerthur was right. The whole climate had changed and society was on the lookout for scapegoats to blame for the poor economic situation. Intolerance was on the rise and the new majority right wing government did nothing but throw oil on the fire.

"If he does move, Philip, I am going with him."

Philip nodded silently. The announcement made him sad. He could not imagine Bill not being around. A painful sense of solitude seized him.

"I don't know what to say…"

Bill visibly made an effort to brighten up again, but his facial expression seemed forced.

"Maybe you should move, too, Philip?"

"Me? I have never thought about that," Philip said stunned.

"Think about it: with your IT expertise it would only be normal that you want to have a stint in a big foreign firm…"

Philip admitted that was right, but he had never felt the need to leave.

"I don't see the point in leaving, Bill."

"Maybe not now, but maybe later." He paused for a moment. "Philip, as much as I admire you for your hacking and what you did earlier today, no one says that you won't get caught. Hacking is illegal and attacking an innocent person is too. The authorities are probably looking for you right now. There's bound to be some CCTV footage of you somewhere."

*

Daniel's large, muscular body was cold and sore from lying on the stone floor. He had a bad headache which seemed to slightly peak with the rhythm of his heartbeat. He had his eyes closed and he was still half asleep.

Sometime later he pulled himself together and glanced at his watch. Six-thirty am. Sunday morning. He suddenly took in his surroundings which jerked him back to consciousness. As he gazed up at the whitewashed Gothic vaulted ceiling, his body shuddered. Against the walls on either side of the narrow room stood dark dusty coffins. "Where on Earth, am I?" He got up on one arm. The narrow room was T-shaped so he could not see where it ended from where he was lying. On the walls, old Baroque tombstones were suspended. Under the layer of dust extravagant carvings served to immortalize the people who had once rested under them.

He felt uncomfortable in these morbid surroundings so he got up and, still a bit dizzy, searched for a way out. He made for the big, wooden door a few meters away. Outside, his eyes had to adjust to the bright morning light. He realized that he stood at a small building attached to a Gothic church which he knew belonged to some foreign congregation. The air was filled with the smell of wet grass and moist stones after the recent rains.

He had gotten totally wasted in a bar the previous night, he recalled. Afterwards, in the street, he had thrown up on his trousers. Rain had started to pour down. How he had come up with the idea of seeking shelter in this chapel, he did not remember. That it was just a stone throw from the last bar he had visited, must have had something to do with it. He pulled the heavy wooden door shut behind him, musing that someone must have forgotten to lock it. His luck.

Daniel felt uncertain as he walked around the church and headed towards the gate in the surrounding wall. Burials had once taken place where the lawn was now. He was careful not to slip on the moist stones scattered around. He was far from sober. Then he stopped, noticing a blond skinny figure with a big dog. "Is that a boy or a girl?" he thought. He then noticed it was a man after all.

The man walked on and disappeared behind the church while Daniel made for the gate. Suddenly he saw that the dog came running back. Daniel took a step back. His body sensed up in anticipation of being attacked by the fierce-looking dog. He slipped on the moist stones and fell onto the wet grass. The dog started to bark even louder now that Daniel was lying down defenselessly.

"Tempest! Come here!" the dog's owner yelled. Tempest promptly responding, wagging her tail.

"I am awfully, sorry" the man said in a clear, high-pitched voice. He bent down to help Daniel up. As Daniel was much larger than him, he had a hard time doing so.

Daniel looked down at himself. His trousers were dirty and his leather jacket was dusty and muddy. The guy stared at him. "Is he checking out my muscles?" Daniel thought. He went to the gym four or five times a week, so he was used to having his body admired. He liked having his body admired.

Tempest sniffed Daniel's hands, who started to pat her and play with her. They seemed to bond immediately and in no time Tempest was jumping playfully up against this stranger. The man had good looks and Philip felt attracted to him. And now that his dog seemed to trust him so much, he decided to try his luck.

"You'd better come with me," he said. "So we can have you cleaned up. I'm Phillip, by the way."

"Daniel."

"Please to meet you, Daniel."

Daniel tagged along. A couple of minutes later, Philip opened a door into an old house. Tempest ran up the stairs ahead of them.

Once inside, Daniel smelled freshly brewed coffee.

"I'd like to go to the loo," he said.

"Sure. The bathroom is over there," Philip pointed at a door at the end of the corridor.

Daniel went inside. He immediately noticed two toothbrushes in a glass. On his way back, he noticed some impressive computer equipment through a door left open into another room.

He sat down on the edge of the couch. Philip brought him a house coat too big to be his own. "If you just give me your trousers, I'll see what I can do," he said and handed Daniel the house coat. He then stepped over to the window silt, pretending to attend to a big green plant while Daniel got his trousers off.

Daniel found Philip's behavior amusing. He was convinced that this little queen would like nothing better than to see him undress.

Philip swiftly disappeared from the room with the dirty trousers while Daniel made himself comfortable on the couch, dressed in the house coat which fit him snugly. His eyes wandered. The room was elegantly furnished. The walls of the apartment were painted white and the floors were made of wood. The sun turned the modest old room into a warm and welcoming place.

Philip came back with a large tray with coffee, mugs, bread, butter and cheese. He took a seat opposite Daniel and placed the tray on the table between them.

"I'm afraid I need to keep you here for a little while. I have just thrown your trousers in the washing machine for a quick wash."

"Cool". Daniel felt like giggling. He was certainly not sober yet.

Sipping coffee from his mug, he noticed that Philip seemed shy all of a sudden as he sat there starring into his mug. He frowned, finding this shyness silly. He took another sip of coffee.

Then Philip locked eyes with Daniel, as if sensing what he had just been thinking. Philip felt awkward, but courageously forced himself to hold Daniel's gaze. Daniel soon looked away. Looking people in the eye had always made Daniel feel uncomfortable.

He looked back at Philip taking in his delicate face with its light complexion. His skin seemed exceptionally light in the sunshine pouring through the window. "Beautiful, but not really a man's face," Daniel thought as he scratched his beard.

"So you had plenty to drink last night, eh? Or was it something else that made you throw up?" Philip asked

"No, just drink. I don't do drugs." Daniel said. For a moment he felt embarrassed remembering how he had never held his drink well. "You know, it happens to all of us, to have too much to drink."

"I rarely drink," Philip answered lightly. "I don't like to get drunk." Daniel felt like asking him what he would then do to party, but refrained.

"Do you live here on your own?"

"What makes you think that I don't?" Philip asked with a slightly amused air.

"I saw two toothbrushes… And then there's this housecoat."

"It's way too big, I know. Yes, I have heard that before. Two tooth brushes because I like to change from time to time, and the housecoat was a gift that I never got around to changing to a smaller size."

Daniel was not sure what to say. He found it very disconcerting that Philip's eyes were pointed directly at him every time he looked his way. So he just smiled thinly and kept quiet. Philip did not mind the silence. He liked quiet mornings.

"You really look tired," he said. "I think you could do with some sleep. Just lean back and take a nap, if you need it. Just put your legs up. Don't mind me."

So Daniel did just that. Philip picked up a newspaper and started reading while Daniel fell asleep.

When Daniel woke up a couple of hours later, his jeans were laid out clean and dry on a chair. The living room was empty, except for Tempest who was asleep in her basket. Quietly, Daniel put on his trousers and went to look for Philip. He heard soft noises coming from the room where he had seen the computers. The door was open. One of the computers was on and Philip sat working.

Daniel gently knocked on the door.

"Eh, I just want to say thank you for fixing my trousers."

Philip got up from his chair and came towards him.

"You're most welcome, anytime."

"He always has a smile in his voice," Daniel thought and he felt a brief flutter of his heart which he resolutely repressed.

"I'd better get home." He turned and walked away with Philip behind him.

In the door Daniel turned to face Philip.

"Thank you for your hospitality and for washing my trousers..." Then he bounded down the stairs and was gone.

Philip closed the door slowly behind Daniel. Then he went to stand at the window looking after the beautiful man who had just left his apartment. He really liked his looks, but somehow he sensed that Daniel was less accepting of him than he had been of his guest. A strong sense of sadness descended on him.

Philip had always been attracted to big guys. He was born looking more like a girl and muscles turned him on more than anything else. Meeting Daniel was a painful reminder of that, a painful memory of unreturned attention felt like someone had just kicked him in the gut. He sometimes hated his body.

He always tried to be friendly at the gym. Anytime he would walk into the locker room, he would greet everyone with a happy "hello." Most of the time his greetings were met by a resounding silence. The silence and lack of any greetings by the other guys in the room always made him feel invisible. Not once had the clique of big iron-pumping guys acknowledged his greetings. "What's wrong with us people?" he would think. "Does a simple 'hello' mean that you are coming on to someone?" He knew that not to be the case, at least not most of the time.

Philip felt equally isolated in gay bars. All the "right" looking guys only had eyes for one another. Mostly on the small screen of their smart phones. He recalled numerous captions such as: "Muscles only! No fems, Black or Asian! No reply, NO INTEREST! Have face pic!"

He mused that the sex applications on the phones were an easy way of not showing any part of your personality, but only your body parts.

*

Philip had been waiting quite a while before a vintage limousine had turned up. *The Baroness* welcomed him from the back seat where he sat smoking a ridiculously slim cigarette. *The Baroness* was tall and slim. Philip was amazed at how lifelike he was in the dimmed light. He kept talking non-stop all the way to the *Naughty Duckling* so Philip wondered if he was on drugs or just terribly nervous.

Upon their arrival at the *Naughty Duckling,* the make-up artist sat Philip down in front of a grand mirror and took a good look at his face.

"No need for heavy make-up here. Your face is beautiful enough as it is."

While she worked on his face, Philip studied the change that gradually took place. When the make-up artist had finished, she fitted a blond wig to his head.

"There!" she said when she met Philip's eyes in the mirror. "If you wore one of these dresses in the street, I bet no one could tell you're not a women. Most of us would kill for those cheekbones."

The both laughed, although Philip was not convinced. Still, he had to admit she had done a fantastic job.

From the dressing room it was clear that the show was now underway. The first girls were already on the catwalk and Mark's presentation was accompanied by applause. Philip felt stiff with terror. He had never done anything like this before. The few times he had convincingly been in drag now seemed light years away. In a minute it was his turn to be scrutinized by the discerning eyes of the fashion industry's eclectic members.

He remembered the tray of cocktails that had been handed around before the show had started. He regretted now that he had refused a drink.

His legs felt uncertain when he entered the catwalk as instructed, wearing a hunter inspired two piece and a hat with a large feather.

"Mark obviously met with hunters while he was in Austria last summer," Philip thought.

Gliding gracefully forward on his high heels towards the end of the catwalk, he kept his eyes over the head of the spectators. In the dimmed lights from the small lamps on the many tables, he could see that the room was full of elegantly dressed people.

After his performance *the Baroness* was ready to go on to display another two piece with more of a trapper look to it.

"Did you see that gorgeous bearded guy at the first table on the right?" she asked Philip.

"No, I am afraid I didn't."

"He was eating you with his eyes, darling. He's got the *hots* for you, as certain as amen in church!"

Philip was relieved that his disguise was pleasing to others. When *the Baroness* walked down the catwalk, Philip stole a glance at the audience from behind the curtain to check out the guy *the Baroness* had been on about. Immediately he caught sight of Daniel! Dressed in a slim cut black suit. "Wow, it makes his muscular body no less sexy," Philip thought. He felt a strong urge to get up and greet him.

Upon her return from the stage, *the Baroness* sent Philip a mischievous wink.

Philip had been appointed to wear the last dress of the evening, which Mark had named *Nuit d'Opéra*. A long black silk dress covered by an enormous cape of cobalt fur fitted with equally sexy shoulder pads.

The audience loved it. Mark was ecstatic that all had gone according to plan. Daniel rose to applaud which brought everyone else out of their seats. Philip stole another glance at him and he saw that he had been recognized before returning his attention to the audience at large.

In the back room the tension had changed to elatedness among the girls and nobody refused the cocktails that were being passed around.

In the midst of the commotion, Bill climbed onto a chair and banging on a champagne cooler brought a momentary quiet to the room.

"Just want to say there's an after party at my place — in drag! Mark says it's okay to use all the dresses."

They all embraced the idea with enthusiasm and soon people were leaving for the party.

"Are you coming with me, Philip?" Bill asked.

"No, just go ahead. After all, you're the host. I'll get a taxi once I am out of this dress."

"No, Philip, you simply must wear that dress. It was the hit of the evening!"

"But I really don't want to be in this dress!"

"You must darling! Don't be such a party pooper! What's wrong with you? You seem upset about something all of a sudden?"

"I don't know what you are talking about… it's nothing…" he answered stunned.

Bill scrutinized Philip for a moment. He was not convinced, but saw no point in pursuing the issue.

"Then, darling, let's not let this 'nothing' get in a way of a fabulous party!

Philip knew that Bill was right. He needed to get out more and mingle with other people.

"Okay then, I'll wear the dress, but go anyway. I just need a moment. I'll catch a taxi."

"I'll have the limo wait for you."

As everyone was heading out, Philip turned and walked back into the *Naughty Duckling* to check if Daniel would still be there. He pulled the curtain aside and signaled to Daniel to come backstage.

He took him by the arm.

"Where are we going?" Daniel asked surprised.

"To a party! Trust me, you won't regret it!"

In the street, Philip walked straight to the vintage limousine. The driver quickly opened the door for them.

"Are we going to drive that thing? Wow!" Daniel said in admiration.

"Yes, it raises the heartbeat of any boy, doesn't it?" Philip replied as he got into the car with some difficulty, hindered by his slim dress and the massive fur cape.

*

It was way past midnight when Philip and Daniel left Bill's place at one of the canals in the center of town. The streets were very quiet. The sound of their footsteps echoed among the houses.

They looked at one another from time to time. Daniel's eyes were warm and expecting. But Philip seemed to be in a pensive mood.

A car approached from behind and slowed down as it passed them, before it turned around the next corner. For a moment, Daniel sensed that Philip was frightened.

"What's wrong, Philip?"

"Have you ever been mugged in the street?"

"No. Have you?"

"Yes. And it happened just like that. A car stopped and some 18-19 year olds jumped out. They attacked me and my friend. We got beaten up, my friend more badly than I … I always have a fright when a car slows down like that."

"I understand." Daniel suddenly realized that he should consider himself lucky never to have been aggressed.

Daniel took Philip's hand and made him stop for a moment. He moved in close to Philip.

"You're are very beautiful in this light, you know?" he said. He never thought he would have heard himself say that to a skinny guy in a dress.

"Thank you!" Philip said. "But I feel ridiculous in this outfit."

"May I kiss you, Madame?" Daniel asked jokingly and before Philip could react, he kissed Philip on the lips. "Are we going to your place?" he whispered. Daniel was surprised by his sudden urge to have sex with Philip who was anything but his type. "Am I that drunk?" he thought slightly confused.

Philip took a step back. Not quite sure of what to make of this tipsy courtship.

"You take it for granted that I want to sleep with a big hunk like you?" he said sharply.

"But don't you?" Daniel could not imagine otherwise. Again he kissed Philip on his mouth. Then waited for an answer.

"I'll make some strong coffee."

*

Tempest was happy to see them, jumping up and down Daniel who started playing with her while Philip turned on the *Nespresso* machine in the kitchen.

When Philip returned with two mugs of coffee, Daniel was nowhere to be seen.

The door to his bedroom was open. He approached and saw that Daniel was sitting under the blankets, resting his broad naked torso against the headrest. His clothes were spread all over the floor. Philip got angry at the nerve of this guy, but he kept quiet. He reminded himself that he was sober while Daniel was probably quite drunk. He went and handed Daniel a mug of coffee. Then he stood back and looked at him coolly.

"Come to bed so we can have coffee and chat, Philip." Daniel padded the pillow next to him. Philip did not move.

Daniel sent him a big smile and put on all his charm.

"Please, come to bed, Daniel." He patted the pillow again.

Philip's resistance melted away and he slowly undressed while he felt Daniel's eyes on his back. The process was not as easy as he would have liked. He hung his dress over a chair and got under the blankets. He had not dared to take off his underwear.

Suddenly, Daniel felt out of balance. Normally, an effeminate male body would have left him cold, but there was something about Philip that turned him on.

"Tell me," he said. "I saw some mighty impressive computers the other day, what do you use them for?"

"I work for an IT company where I am head of a department that develops software, you know guiding systems and applications for phones and such."

Daniel was speechless for a moment. Then he started laughing. His entire big body moved in the process.

"I'm sorry," he said, trying to suppress his laughter, but that only made things worse.

"What's so funny about that?" Philip wanted to know.

Daniel reached for Philip's hand and placed it on his chest.

"Imagine! Here I am in bed with the prettiest little queen in town and then he turns out to be an IT genius."

Philip swiftly withdrew his hand and turned his head away. "This guy has no idea," he thought. "How difficult it can be to be a feminine gay man. And the worst of it is that his own kind is often the worst. It is so much easier when you look like the ideal." Then he sat up with his back to Daniel.

Despite his drunkenness, Daniel knew he had gone too far. So he put his mug down.

"Sorry, I didn't mean to upset you," he whispered gently. He got closer and started to massage Philip's shoulders. When Philip got more relaxed, Daniel sat down with one leg on either side of Daniel's body. Then he embraced him. He held him tight to his body and kissed his ear, running his nose through his curly hair.

*

A couple of days later at the gym, Daniel studied his muscular shaven body in the mirror wall in the locker room. He had just come out of the shower and picked up his towel to go to the sauna. It was still early and few people were in the gym, except for a couple of early birds like himself doing their workout before going to the office. He stopped for a moment. "My chest and biceps are coming along nicely, aren't they," he thought. He had always had skinny legs so he had compensated that by building up a broad chest and large biceps.

He did not have a lot of time, but he always took some time to relax in the sauna. He had a hectic job so he needed moments of peace. He closed his eyes to meditate. Just to clear his mind.

He set out on his usual routine: slowly breathing in and out. Whenever his mind wandered off, he brought it back to his breathing. Images of Philip's brown eyes and handsome face kept emerging. He admitted to himself that he had enjoyed the party and the night with him, but he felt confused about it. A little embarrassed even. He was one of those big guys who hang out only with the other big guys.

No fems! As the saying goes. He did not want to be seen in intimate company with someone like Philip. No, Philip was going to be his little secret for a while. Only until he found someone new in his own league. Dismayed he broke off his routine, sensing his erection under his towel.

*

"No, no, Daniel" Bill corrected him. "It's not carnival! It's a bad taste party. There's a fine line between the two."

Daniel looked doubtfully at himself in the mirror. The red and green rowing suit certainly accentuated his body, but the colors made him look like a piece of candy. Philip and Bill grinned and seemed pleased with his attire. Both had been to a shop run by the Salvation Army and had found two black fur coats which they now wore over identical green kimonos and green wigs.

As they left for the party in a taxi, Daniel wore a jogging suit over his costume. He felt embarrassed. He could not comprehend how Philip and Bill just seemed to merge with their garments and become two different people altogether. He noticed how the taxi driver kept looking at them in the rear mirror. Bill produced a small bottle of whisky from his handbag and offered his friends a drink. Philip kindly refused, but Daniel took a big gulp. Bill finished the small bottle off. As they got out of the taxi, Daniel noticed that the taxi driver reached for a tag with some Arabic written on it. He kissed it as he looked after them with disgust. Daniel thought he heard him hiss the words *Allah ak-bar*. He frowned.

The party was in full swing when Daniel entered, dressed in his rowing suit. This apartment was a huge place on the top of a former factory. It had wonderful views over the harbor. This neighborhood offered great spaces if you dared to invest on the basis of a trend. The owner obviously did.

He examined the crowd of people. They were dressed in the most diverse and tasteless attires he had ever seen gathered at the same spot. As he moved in among the people, he noticed how they eyed his body and made room for him to pass. This usual reaction made him feel good and he relaxed a little. A waiter came up to him and offered him cocktails from a tray. All were either green or blue.

"What are they?" he asked.

"Poison Ivy or Mouth Wash, Sir". Daniel thought the waiter's voice belonged to a girl, but could not tell for sure whether it was a boy or a girl. He picked a poison ivy, but before he could ascertain his sex, the waiter was gone. Then, on the opposite side of the room, he caught sight of Bill and Philip in their green wigs talking to a massive man wearing a West African garment in light blue, black and white. So he made for them.

"Ah, there you are!" Philip said and dragged Daniel gently into their small group by the elbow.

"Daniel - may I introduce you to Noël, our host? Noël, this is my friend Daniel," Philip said.

At that moment, another waiter walked up to them and offered them a tray with hotdogs. Daniel wondered if hotdogs were all they were going to have to eat. Noël waved him away and took a step towards Daniel. He was a head taller than Daniel so he was a real giant.

"Well, hello!" he said in a deep voice. "You're certainly the best piece of eye candy around. I am so pleased to meet you. Do make yourself at home and leave your troubles outside!" He offered a hand which made Daniel's hand seem tiny.

"Thank you very much!" answered Daniel and he shook the giant's hand.

"So are you going to row for us or do you have some other entertainment up that suit?" Noël said loudly.

"What do you mean?"

"All guests are encouraged to entertain the others. The more tasteless the better," Noël continued to explain. "These green girls over here", he said, pointing with his chin at Philip and Bill, "will no doubt sing some opera for us. God help us!" He chuckled. Daniel was stunned. No one had told him that he was supposed to entertain anybody. He looked angrily in the direction of Philip. He should have warned him.

But before he could react, Noël seemed to have lost interest in him and looked at something behind him. "Hush my babies", he said in a booming voice. "I discern that the German *Gräffin* wants our attention!"

Daniel turned around. Everyone's attention was focused on an elderly tall person dressed like some late German film star whom he could not quite place. The *Gräffin* climbed onto a chair in her long dress, helped by the waiter who had served Daniel.

General applause in the room broke out as the Gräffin rose precariously on top of the chair and sent hand kisses to the guests. With a gracious movement she placed her index finger on her lips to quiet everyone. Accepting a cocktail the waiter offered her, she stroke her long pearl necklace.

"Berlin, Berlin!" the *Gräffin* began. People broke out in applause and cried out in encouragement. "They seem to know the text," Daniel thought in amazement.

"Berlin! Berlin! Einmal die Hauptstad des dritten Reiches!
Dann eine einsame Stadt in einem fremden Lande!
Berlin! Berlin! Die Mutter der Untergrunddekadenz,
Jetzt eine vergammelte Frau mit offenen Beinen!
Berlin! Berlin! Warte auf mich!"

"Berlin! Berlin! Warte auf mich!" the spectators shouted as they joined the *Gräffin* in a toast.

"Wonderful darling! Absolutely wonderful!" Noël said and he offered a hand to help the *Gräffin* down the chair.

Turning to face the crowd, his strong voice drowned their voices. "Babies, it's now time for dinner!" He made a grand gesture. The double doors opened and the guests poured into the next room. "I expect some entertaining speeches during dinner!" he shouted.

Philip darted forwards to lead Daniel by the hand. Daniel brusquely withdrew his hand, hoping that no one had noticed Philip's move. Then he started to move with the crowd into the next room. Philip was stunned and hurt and it took him a moment before he followed Daniel. "Have I got it all wrong?" he thought. He had the impression his heart was about to burst. "How can he be so tender all night and then shun me like this?"

Bill watched his longtime friend trail indecisively behind Daniel into the dining area with pity. "The *overture* to this party was too rosy," he mused sadly. There was nothing he wanted more than for Philip finally to be happy with another man.

*

The cool autumn air met them as they stepped out of the opera house. They all welcomed the chill. It had been very warm inside the theatre.

"This woolen jacket is a lot warmer than you'd think," Bill said. His breath was clearly visible in the cool air.

"So no need for anyone to keep you warm, eh?" Daniel remarked teasingly.

"You never know," Bill said happily.

"Come," Bill said and he steered Philip across the square with his arm around his shoulder. They walked ahead of Daniel in the direction of *Siegfried and Joel*. Philip cozied up to his old friend. Daniel felt a fleeting moment of jealousy seeing them like that, but he was not so sure what he really wanted. Did he really want to be seen in public with Philip that way? Philip looked back over his shoulder and sent Daniel a mischievous grin.

"Tell me: any idea how many cakes you've eaten in that place, Philip?" Bill questioned teasingly.

"What a dreadful question! A daunting number, I can tell you."

Suddenly the ground shook under them and there was the sound of an explosion and splintering glass. Philip stumbled and fell to the ground. A small piece of glass had cut into his temple. It was only by a miracle that Bill and Daniel had not been hit by any flying glass. Bill was coughing wildly. They all felt like standing close to a pyre. Their lungs started to hurt from breathing in the hot smoky air.

In front of them *Siegfried and Joel* was engulfed in flames. Philip cried out in sheer terror. His voice was drowned in the piercing screams coming from the café. They stood transfixed to the spot, paralyzed by the sight of people trapped in the fire. Some got out, screaming in agony with their hair and clothes on fire. Throwing themselves about like panicking animals.

The cars on the square stopped, but few drivers were courageous enough to get out and run towards the burning people with their fire extinguishers.

Soon they heard sirens, echoing violently against the buildings. The flashing blue lights emphasized the madness of the moment.

As the fire engines entered the square, they came to an almost standstill as they were cut off by the traffic. Slowly, painfully slowly it seemed, they got close enough to get the water hoses out.

Daniel overcame his inability to move. He got down on his knees and took Philip in his arms. He held him firmly against his own shaking body. Around them, hundreds of people from the opera had gathered. Looking on silently in horror. Had this happened place a little later *Siegfried and Joel* would have been full of people dropping in for an after opera cocktail.

After a while, the heat seemed to abate somewhat and the surviving victims were on their way to hospital, leaving the task of dealing with the dead corpses strewn in front of the former café to the remaining ambulance crew.

"Bill!" Daniel screamed. "Let's get out of here!" They helped Philip to the car parked nearby. Daniel and Philip got in the back. Bill took off. No one said anything. Slowly Bill maneuvered his car away from the clogged streets around the opera. With each meter the world grew more peaceful, although it had changed forever.

*

Daniel led Philip to the bathroom and sat him down on the toilet.

With blood running down his face, Philip looked scary. Daniel held his head still and examined him closer. The glass had only hit his skin superficially without lodging in the temple. He was relieved that Philip was not seriously hurt.

"Have you got some disinfectant?" he asked.

"There's a spray in the closet above the wash basin."

Daniel opened the closet to search for the spray.

Philip felt dizzy and his body was tense. The wound hurt like hell and blood was dripping onto his shirt. "What had happened?" His mind was churning:" We could have been killed if we had walked just a little faster!"

Daniel found the disinfectant spray, some cotton and bandages.

While clearing the wound, he studied Philip's face. He was clearly very upset.

Then Bill entered the bathroom with a glass of brandy.

"Here!" he said. "Have a good sip, Philip. It'll do you good."

Philip had never been a drinker so when he took a sip, he felt the strong liquid radiate throughout his body. He started to cough.

"Will do me g- g- good…?" he coughed.

"Yeah! You see? It got you talking!" Bill flashed a big smile at him.

"Guys, we could have been killed! All of us!" Philip said.

Daniel, at a loss for words, gazed at the floor.

"But we didn't!" Bill replied friendly, but firmly. "Don't go there, Philip. We weren't meant to die to day!"

Philip was afraid to close his eyes. He still saw the images of people coming out of the café with their hair and clothes on fire. He kept silent.

"I'm going to check the news," Bill suddenly said and left the bathroom.

While Daniel put the bandages and disinfectant back in the cupboard, he heard the sound of the television being turned on in the living room. He looked at his watch. "Time for the late night news," he said. "Come." He helped Philip up and they too went to the living room.

"...at least 15 people are reported dead in the explosion. A similar number are at hospital in a critical condition," the news anchor announced gravely. "The police are investigating the possible causes for the explosion. Currently, they are focusing on a possible gas leak in the old building. Meanwhile, on the internet, several organizations are claiming responsibility for the bombing. Notably the Movement for Societal Cleansing. MSC states that its objectives are to purge society from the homosexual degeneration. It warns that today's action is just the beginning of a series of such cleansing actions. Likewise, several extremist Moslem organizations equally claim credit for the bombing, or at least welcome it..."

"Turn that off!" Philip burst out. Bill frowned. But when he saw how upset Philip was, he did as ordered. The room fell silent for a moment.

"Argh!" Daniel shouted after a few moments. "Gas leak, my foot! I cannot have this. Those fucking morals and

Muslims are not going to tell me how to live my life! We have got to do something!"

Philip nodded slightly in agreement.

"What would you have us do?" said Bill. "We have no idea of who they are?"

"Oh, I'm sure that the government's youth section is involved in this," Daniel retorted.

"Dangerous allegations against a democratically elected party," Philip noted softly, but loud enough for all to hear.

Bill's mobile phone rang. He had left it in the kitchen so he went to answer it. A moment later he was back.

"That was Winerthur. He has just heard the news. He is freaking out with worry. He's in a taxi on his way home from the airport. He wants me to go home, too."

"Why don't you ask him to come over here then?" Philip asked sharply.

Bill looked pensively at Philip for a moment.

"Maybe Philip. But I would also like to go home. To *my* home now..."

"Yes, of course... you're perfectly right... sorry."

As Bill left, Daniel wanted to go out, too.

"I need some air," he stated bluntly.

Alone with Tempest, Philip stood at the window. He saw Bill's car leave while beautiful Daniel briskly walked away in the other direction. Towards the gay bars! Philip was in inner turmoil and felt abandoned. He could understand that Bill wanted to go home to his lover, but what about Daniel? "Has he just used me?" his mind droned on. He felt like crying, but suppressed the urge. "Why does he show such gentleness when he cleans my wounds and then just walks out on me to go to the gay bars?" His disappointment created a piercing pain in his stomach. He felt utterly lonely. Silently tears were running down his face.

He stood there for a long time. Breathing slowly in and out, trying to calm his mind and to get some distance from the horrific experience. When his inner turmoil had somewhat abated, he went into his office and turned on his computers to have a look at the postings on the internet. And to see what he could do about them.

*

One evening, a few days later his doorbell rang. Philip looked at the clock. It was almost ten pm. He did not expect visitors at this time of the day. He had entertained the idea of an early night.

The doorbell rang again. Very insistently and repeatedly. From the kitchen, he heard Tempest bark agitatedly.

Philip got up and peeped through the spyhole. As he saw Daniel standing outside the door, he jerked back. "What does he want?" Philip thought. "Not a sign of him since he abandoned me last time!" He felt like pretending he was not at home. But Daniel rang the doorbell again and knocked on the door, too.

"Philip, open up the door!" he shouted in an agitated voice. "You must be home, you have got all the lights on!"

Hesitantly Philip opened the door and Daniel barged in. Philip noticed with a fright that he had a bad bruise on his chin.

"What happened?" Philip turned pale.

Daniel proceeded without a word to the bathroom and took a close look in the mirror. "Only a bad scratch," he said. "Nothing serious." Nevertheless, he got the disinfectant out and cleaned his bruise.

Philip stood in the doorway, moving from one leg to the other, with mounting frustration over Daniel's behavior. "I think I have had enough of this guy," he suddenly realized. "Barging in like that, and now he even doesn't bother to answer a simple question!"

Meanwhile, Daniel fitted a small bandage. "I was in a fight," he said in a low voice. He was in no mood for questions.

"Yes, I can see that, Daniel." Philip suppressed his anger and told himself to be patient. "Maybe Daniel is just shocked," he tried to convince himself. He wanted to ask whom he had been in a fight with, but he refrained as he saw how closed Daniel seemed.

Daniel looked up. Then he came forward and gave Philip a timid hug before squeezing past him into the living room. Philip trailed behind him with an exasperated expression on his face.

"Mind if I help myself to a drink?" Daniel deliberately did not look at Philip.

"Go ahead..." Philip answered icily.

Daniel sat down in the sofa. Philip, too, sat down. Daniel gulped his drink down.

"So, what happened?" Philip asked firmly. "I see you've taken quite a beating."

"A few of my friends and I decided that the youth organization offices needed a little sorting out... so we broke in and destroyed a few things... It's amazing how easy it is to tear things apart once you've started, you know."

Sitting face to face with Daniel, Philip's resolve faltered at the sight of the bandage. He had seen the nasty bruise. Now his gentler side got the upper hand again.

"You could have been seriously hurt," Philip whispered. He leaned forward and ever so lightly touched Daniel's bruised chin while he searched for his gaze. Daniel looked away. He took another sip of his drink and closed his eyes. "The caress felt good after all," he thought.

"And while you were *sorting out things*, you got in a fight?" Philip wanted to know.

"Yes. A few youth members showed up and caught us red-handed. They fought ferociously, but we managed to get out of there." He felt proud to have done the right thing.

"That was an unnecessarily dangerous thing to do."

"*That was an unnecessarily dangerous thing to do*," mimicked Daniel. "No, it was not an unnecessarily dangerous thing to do! It was *the* right thing to do!"

Philip withdrew his hand as if it had just been burned and looked disapprovingly at Daniel who met his glance with hostility.

"I'm doing the right thing, Philip," he shouted. "What are you doing? Or Bill? Mourning that you have nowhere decent to eat chocolate cake these days?"

Philip had not expected Daniel to sink so low. "You don't know what you are saying," he answered irritably.

"Oh, I don't know what I am saying, am I?" Daniel countered. "The most progressive thing I have seen you and Bill do was to get into a taxi in a couple of grandma furs and green kimonos! I bet the only reason the taxi driver did not say anything to the two of you was because I was there to protect you!" Daniel was on his feet now ready to stand his ground.

"So you don't think Bill and I can protect ourselves!? I'll tell you what: It was Bill who was with me all those years ago when we got mugged in the street!"

Daniel barely saw it coming when Philip somehow made him fall over so swiftly that he could not defend himself. He fell heavily on his back onto the carpet. Philip was on top of him and placed all his weight on Daniel's shoulders. They locked eyes and Philip could see Daniel's amazement.

"A nice police man taught us some self-defense afterwards!" he shouted in Daniel's face. "So that we would never be defenseless!"

From behind the closed kitchen door, Tempest was barking violently.

"Enough! Calm down!" Philip said to himself. "Let's just get Daniel out of the door without further ado. He's not worth it" He knew he would be no good against Daniel's strength without the element of surprise.

It dawned on Daniel that he might just have met his match. Groggily he got on his knees and reached for Philip's hand, but Philip left him to get up on his own. He sent Philip a boyish smile. "He can't even bring himself to say that he's sorry," Philip thought. He felt hurt, but he was also relieved, accepting that he would be better off without him.

Philip had now calmed down so he took Daniel's hand, who hoped that this was a sign that they were going to make up in bed. All the action had made him horny.

But when Daniel was on his feet, he led him into his study where he sat him down in front of the computer screens. Daniel felt disorientated.

"Are we going to play a computer game?" he asked awkwardly.

Philip keyed in an address and the website of the government came on screen.

"Yes, something like that... let me show you something...have you ever played *troll*?"

"Troll?"

"'*Troll* is what you play on computers without any identification – a bit like sending anonymous letters. I'm sure there are a few things you'd like to tell our government, no? How you hate everything they stand for?"

Suddenly they heard the doorbell ring and someone pounding on the door!

"Open up!" an angry male voice rang out. "We know you're in there!" The banging was relentless. Tempest started barking again.

Daniel stared at Philip who quickly keyed in a few commands. The computer started to shot down.

"What are you doing?" Daniel whispered?

"An emergency erasure of the hard disk!" Philip hissed.

Then Philip briskly got up and opened a cupboard under the window silt. There was a heavy rope. "All these old houses come with fire precautions," Philip said and he beckoned Daniel to come to the window. As he threw the rope out of the window, Daniel noticed that it was attached to a hook in the wall."

"Hurry, Daniel. Get yourself out of here."

"But what about you?"

"I have done nothing illegal. I'll face whatever comes..."

Sabine Sur

Invisibility is an acquired taste

I always look at people in the eye when I am rapping, because people do not refuse eye contact in the metro. They are only too glad that someone has noticed them, and they feel that they have to pay attention. Yet there's this girl who keeps reading some papers, right in front of me.

Her back is all hunched over and her head is all bent and her hair is falling over her face but there's something about her that catches my attention. She's reading a text with lines highlighted in bright orange and I can't help but think in a flash, while singing my lines, that she's an actress, probably famous, famous enough to be on the cover of a magazine, pretending to be just like everyone else in the underground. The young woman next to her took off her earphones when I came in and now she is looking at me with enjoyment and something like admiration. I am a good rapper. I stare at her instead.

Then I take the time to meet the eye of an older man with a bright green jumper and a light brown blazer – men and women are so obsessed with their clothes here. He is looking back at me too, with amazement. My beatbox is pounding its tune and I am going effortlessly through the fast pace, giving it all my energy, enjoying every bit of it, as usual. At the end, when I do my round in the car, four passengers give me coins: this is a great success.

When I get down at the next station, my uncle is waiting to collect my cash. My cousin is holding his leg. She's wearing her cute pink frilly dress; when the next car pulls in, she is going to do her first round of begging. 'I'll teach you another song tonight' I tell her to cheer her up, and she nods shyly.

As I walk down the corridors of the metro to make my connection, I play the last lines of my rap in my head – *I'm Cosmina, and I'm not vanilla/This is my song and you can think it's wrong/It can make you glad or it can make you mad/I'm here to stay and I will make my way,* and I wonder how I can make it better. Then I think about that hunched girl in the car.

I really think that she is a star trying to be incognito. When I imagine my future, I see myself big and famous – admired, with lots of fans, very beautiful and pampered, having crossed the river from nobodiness to fame one stepping stone at a time – but now I'm wondering if it wouldn't be nice to be so famous that I would just want to hide myself and try to go unnoticed in the metro. I think that would be just the neatest thing.

To step out of my limo and its driver, hiding my designer clothes and my world-renowned face under a shabby coat, and just hop on to the underground, hoping that nobody will recognize me.

Dimitris Politis

Do not forget to feed the dog...

My eye sockets shrank as I focused hard to look out through the blurred window. Countless droplets of moisture had stuck stubbornly to the internal surface of the glass, blocking any visual contact with the outside. Each time their weight became unable to resist gravity, they let themselves run slowly down like thick tears, forming dirty little pools on the dusty surface of the sill. An obvious feel of neglect filled the room. Its naked walls painted in a shiny green oil paint brought to mind a room from a slaughterhouse refrigerator. I could almost visualise the hooks with frozen carcasses hanging from the ceiling.

The dim light of the naked bulb hanging from the ceiling was barely enough to illuminate the sorry state of everything. "Maybe it's not so bad this way, the less one can see the better", I said to myself. I lowered my head and looked at my hands in desperation. The fact that I was still wearing my heavy coat and my black leather gloves, did not prevent the cold from penetrating deep my bones and making them hurt. That wretched chair I was sitting on did not help either. I had been trying hard to balance uncomfortably on it, fearing it could dissolve into a thousand pieces any minute: its rickety legs were cracking menacingly at my slightest movement. Obliged to sit in such an unnatural posture and uncomfortable position for a while, I felt most of my bones numb and ever more susceptible to the hostile freeze of the place.

I turned and looked at the iron bed next to me. Beneath a pile of thick blankets, an undetermined mass, like a tangle of cast-off laundry, was sticking above the mattress. It reminded me of our clumsy attempts to trick our parents when we were children, when we stuffed a pile of clothes under the blanket and shouted in panic that some stranger was lying beneath the blankets on our beds. They played along even though they understood immediately our little trick, pretending they were seriously concerned at first, and then bursting into laughter as they forgave us tenderly one more rascal act.

"Everything okey mother?" I asked worryingly the unattractive shape protruding from the bed. Sticking out from the thick stack of blankets, messy locks of uncombed gray hair revealed beneath them two scared eyeballs that shone in the scarse light. She responded to me with a lifeless, vacant look, letting a dead, crooked smile shape her face. It was so blatantly obvious: there was not a single human emotion behind that smile. More like a twitch of her face it was.

"Do not forget to feed the dog!" she replied in that eerie voice. It barely sounded like a proper phrase. It came out of her like a groan. I jumped up. Rushing in fury out of the hospital room, I threw myself onto the deserted corridor of the second floor. The only floor nurse in charge noticed me from across the other end. She moved swiftly towards me in the half-darkness like a shadow, wrapped-up in a thick woolen sweater and a hand-knitted scarf.

"Can I help you, sir? Have you got a problem? Is everything alright?" she approached me cautiously.

"Yes, I do have a problem! A big problem! This situation is totally unacceptable! We are in the middle of winter, yet there isn't a hint of heating in this damned clinic!" I shouted back at her, my voice trembling, despite my effort to keep control over its intensity and my overflowing anger. "It is so utterly unacceptable and cruel to have left all patients in the psychiatric ward at the mercy of the snow and their destiny! You, the nurses and doctors have taken an oath to protect, cure and relieve patients, for goodness sake!... Do something!!" I protested, almost choked by my feelings.

"I am really sorry, sir...You are very right..." the words came tired out of her mouth. She turned her head towards the floor to avoid my look. "Unfortunately, we cannot do anything... You know ... We follow strict orders. Our oil supply and our finances allow our clinic to be heated only an hour a day ... radiators usually turn on during the morning for sixty minutes, when patients get up, so they are able to wash a little and use the bathroom. As you can see, most of them spend the day in their beds. We try to monitor them as closely as we can. We try to distribute hot water bottles frequently... We make sure they are protected from the cold, that they remain as warm as possible and comfortable under their blankets... We try, we try our best..."

I had been watching her in silent rage as she was struggling with her apology. Before she had the time to finish her last phrase, I had already turned my back to her with a sudden movement and walked away. She was left standing dumbstruck in the empty corridor as I rushed back to my mother's room. There was nothing more she could say, there was nothing more I could ask. Her reply was no news to me. I knew she was telling the truth. Neither had I any illusions that my strong protests would bring any results. I just had to somehow vent my anger, to externalise from deep inside me that sense of frustration that was drowning me.

I returned to my creaking chair. It complained again with another groan as it felt my weight upon it. I bent over to grab my mother's hand and try to caress it. She pulled it quickly under the blankets. Perhaps the strange feeling of my leather gloves was on her flesh frightened her.

"Do not forget to feed the dog!" she deeply exhaled pronouncing the same seven words with as much clarity as she had left in her destroyed mind. With as much reason she was permitted to have since she was struck by that cursed Alzheimer's disease. Despite our repeated family pleas, doctors were adamant: her advanced condition would make her dangerous to herself and to others outside the clinic. She should remain permanently hospitalised and under heavy sedation, there was no question about that.

I tried to give her back a smile.

"Do not forget to feed the dog! Do not forget to feed the dog!" She kept repeating over and over, like some sad monologue of the absurd.

The clock dial seemed frozen in time. It was the same each time I visited her: time felt motionless, minutes and seconds passed so painfully slowly.

Eventually, I decided it was time to leave. I took off my gloves and bent over her head. I kissed her tenderly on the forehead and stroked her hair; putting extra care not to touch her flesh directly with my cold hands and give her a shock. They must have felt like blocks of ice on bare skin.

"Do not forget to feed the dog!" she whispered one last time starring into the void.

"It's OK mother. Don't worry. I have just fed him!" I replied loudly, trying to hold back the tears burning behind my eyes. They had accumulated in dozens and they were pressing terribly to escape, threatening to deluge my face any moment now. I turned and headed quickly towards the door, resolutely not looking back.

Seconds later, I unlocked my car and collapsed heavy on the driver's seat. I turned the engine on to warm it up and switched on the warm air full blast. I pinned my gaze in the thick dark mass that prevailed outside the car's windshield.

"My mother has been an honest, decent human being who worked hard all her life, trying to help her family and everybody else" I thought. "After thirty five years of loyal service in a hospital; she received a meagre pension from State Social Security Scheme. Alas, she had not been allowed to enjoy her retirement - the Alzheimer's disease hit her unexpectedly just one year later. Its development was rampant, menacing her brain relentlessly. Now with her mind just about dead, she spends her last days on a dirty mattress in a decrepit state psychiatric hospital. She has been abandoned there to rot with the bare minimum of care. Completely let-down by an over-indebted, paralysed state, incapable of protecting those who need it most: the weak and sick. Thrown in a freezing chamber like a dead carcass, paying dearly not for her own mistakes, but for the mistakes of others... Without the care that she truly deserves, without access to even the basics such as heating amidst deep winter. Is this progress? Is this civilization? Where are our values? Our humanity?" I wondered as a silent sob shook my body.

"Why does *she* have to pay for this? Why? And in such a cruel and unacceptable manner? Why does she have to pay for the failures of our society? Why does she have to pay at any cost for the cruel and merciless money-games of those driven by greed and an unbridled thirst for power and wealth?"

A new sob shook me. I wiped my eyes hurriedly, put the car into first gear and pressed my foot firmly on the accelerator. The car disappeared quickly in the deserted roads somewhere in the icy northern suburbs of the city.

—Athens, Greece, winter 2012

Barbara Mariani

Antonio's room

Antonio's room was the perfect refuge from distress. Unlike most people in the office, he had refused to stick to the company's Danish minimalist style and had wanted to reshape his space from A to Z. The walls had been painted in faint turquoise and recessed lights finely shaped like shells had been placed on three corners of the room.

An Artemide floor lamp illuminated his antique American oak writing desk and an Art Deco sofa in ash pink was placed on the far end of the room. There were no other pieces of furniture in the room, except a modern glass coffee table that could be turned into a dining table on occasion and an Indonesian boat-shaped bookshelf.

The boat came from a tiny fishing village on one of the Indonesian islands where he had stopped during his long world journey on his Vespa in the late '70s. An old fisherman had turned the boat he had built with his hands forty years earlier, into a piece of furniture that he had entrusted to the village school.

A night fire had half destroyed the school few weeks before Antonio arrived in the village and the boat, miraculously saved by the fisherman himself during the fire, had been returned to its original place outside the fisherman's hut. As a sign of trust and friendship, he gave it to Antonio, to whom he had told the story of his life in a semi-comprehensible language stretched throughout several evenings spent under the stars, sitting on the boat outside the house and drinking Wedang Jahe.

When the man gave Antonio the boat, he told him he was happy to know that somewhere on the other side of the planet, a piece of his life on earth would be guarded and remain precious for several years on after his death.

It had taken Antonio two months to organise the shipping to the mainland and from there the delivery to his loft in San Francisco Bay. He hadn't left the Archipelago until he had seen the boat safely shipped on a cargo to the States.

A world globe marking with small Vespas all the places he had touched during his adventure was standing on one side of his desk. Hanging on the wall in front of the desk, exactly at the same height of his look, an original black and white photo of Marcello Mastroianni.

The Italian style icon was bending on the railing of a hotel balcony on the Riviera in the late '60s, wearing a double-breast striped suit and a black tie and holding the inseparable cigarette in his hand. The picture had perfectly captured the actor's secret. A perfect balance between the strict and the informal, an aura of mystery and aloofness, where the corrosive irony of the corrugated brow was soothed by the warmth of his compassionate look "I have seen and lived through all things human..." Antonio had never revealed how he had got hold of the picture.

Patrick ten Brink

The Bird Man

One night hundreds of years ago, in the time of the Samurai, a young man, stripped to his waist, was training at sword fighting in the mountain forests. The moon and the stars came out and he continued to swing and thrust his sword, tracing paths of sharp, reflected, light through the air, leaping light-footed, a silent dance of muscle and steel.

He heard the calls of unfamiliar birds, sat down and laid his sword on his lap. The young man sat under the stars listening to the bird song. He stared into the sky, at the passing of the night stars, trying to recognise and read the constellations – he saw the two-sided drum and remembered his father, a village musician cut down by thieves. Hand on his sword, he searched the heavens, spotting the snake. He breathed in deeply and out, now finding the dragon, the bird of paradise, and the Phoenix.

He leapt up and launched back into his training.

A drop of sweat splashed on his shining arm. Sword held thrusting into the sky, he peered at his other arm where the drop landed – wet spots on his skin matched a star constellation at his sword's tip. He looked at his sword arm and surveyed the star patterns above. Again, stars mirrored the dots on his arm. He inspected his stomach, stripped down further to bare his legs and sought echoes of bright star constellations traced in the dark spots on his skin.

He stared at the moon and the stars and back to his body.

A bird landed on a rock near him but beyond his reach. He had never seen such a bird before. It had a curious shape – a small white owl's face with green eyes, a magpie's body, and long blue tail feathers. It sang, beautifully.

He held his arm out.

The bird flew to him, landed on his wrist, cocked its head, looked him in the eye and flew off.

The young man watched the creature fly into the bamboo forest. His gaze drifted to his arm and he saw the bird traced in dots on his skin. He stood up, swore to himself, picked up his sword and practiced more earnestly than before. He was angry with himself for imagining patterns in the birthmarks on his skin -- a Samurai does not lose focus.

He slept fitfully that night, visited by dreams of stars, birds and song. He woke early and trained all day, this time near the river. So deep in training was he that he did not see the villagers and travellers who passed. Towards the late afternoon, a boat drifted past, and he heard a girl's voice say to her friend on the boat – 'Did you see the beauty spots along the boy's arm? They looked like the outline of a bird, a glowing bird.' Her friend laughed. 'Goodbye bird-man,' they called after him.

He was shaken out of his training and called out, 'I will be a Samurai, I will honour the sword, honour the code, honour my family's name!'

The boat was now almost lost behind bamboo plumes that cast shadows across the river; the girls giggled and one said, 'Sing, bird-man; may your voice be as powerful as your silver sword.' And they were gone.

The young man was confused. Girls did not speak to trainee Samurai like that. He looked up at the hot sun and wondered whether he was training too hard and imagining things. He dived into the river and swam to cool off.

He lay on the grass and dreamed of his future as a Samurai, of becoming a guardian of his village. His dreams mixed with stories of water spirits. He woke up, cold; the sun was sinking into the horizon and the bird from the night before stood in the bamboo watching him.

He called to the bird, but it flew away, casting a song to him as it left.

The young man trained, but every day he saw the bird and watched it fly into the forest. Curious, he started to explore the forest, the first day cutting only minutes from his training. The next day he ventured further, searched for longer. On the third day, he came across an old man in a black kimono painting a bird on the bark of a tree.

The young man bowed and asked, 'I've been looking for that bird. Do you know where it flew?'

The old man, tears in his eyes, said, 'It flew to the land beyond ours. She was my songbird. I will miss her song so.'

The young man bowed again and said, 'My name is Akio. Can I be of service? I could seek the bird for you.'

The painter frowned. 'Where she has gone no one can travel. But please do me the honour and join me for tea,' he added, shuffling to a small wooden house lodged between two trees. 'It would give me pleasure to talk to you of my songbird. I like to take tea out here under the cherry tree. Listen to the songs of the forest while I get the tea.'

Akio sat cross-legged on a patch of moss under the tree, white petals dotting the green carpet and closed his eyes.

'Ah you sit under my favourite tree. I always think the blossoms will rise again like butterflies and return to the branches.' He held out a cup of green tea to Akio. 'Thank you for honouring an old man. It is not every day a Samurai joins me.'

'I am only training, hoping to find a teacher to guide me in the way of the sword. And you are a master painter, so the honour is all mine.'

The old painter smiled and rolled up his sleeve, revealing a tattoo of the bird.

'She is so beautiful!' exclaimed Akio. 'It is as if she is there, sleeping on your arm.'

'You see. She is gone, but stays with me. Listen.' He raised the tattoo to the young man's ear.

Akio heard a faint song of the bird, the same call that the bird had sent him on the first day. 'That song!' Astonished, he rolled up his own sleeve and showed the spots that made the shape of a bird.

The old man drew in his breath sharply and clapped his hands. 'You are the one I have been waiting for,' he said. 'My soul is comforted that you are here. Please come.' He slid open the paper doors to his home and showed Akio inside. Bird paintings covered the walls from floor to ceiling. Dozens of pots made of cut bamboo, each full of paintbrushes, stood around the room, and in the corner, near the fire and teapot, lay a row of fine needles and clay pots of coloured inks. He touched the spots on Akio's arm, pointed at his tattoo and the needles.

Akio bowed. 'I have no money that I can give for the honour of one of your beautiful tattoos.'

'That the bird chose you is enough. Please sit, Akio-san. This may hurt,' he said holding the needles in the flame, waving them in the air and dipping one into the inkpot. 'Give me your arm.'

'To be a Samurai, I need to learn that pain is nothing.'

'Be careful what you learn, Akio-san.'

Two hours later, Akio had a beautiful bird tattoo on his arm, the star-like beauty spots forming the beak, wingtips, feet, breast and eyes. The old man offered him fresh tea, and they sat together, each holding the cup in two hands and blowing across the steaming surface. They drank in silence.

Tea finished, the old tattoo-man whistled.

A bird flew and landed on his arm. 'Raise your arm, Akio-san.'

Akio did as instructed, and the bird flew to his arm.

'She is yours now. But there is a secret about this bird, and some other birds...'

'What is it?'

'You and I can see this bird; others do not. If they are lucky, they hear the song but never see the bird. It has passed from here, and only rare people -- painters, poets, musicians and monks can see it.'

'But I will be a Samurai!'

'If that is the case, you will be a special Samurai. But there is more than defending honour with the sword, protecting with steel.'

'I will not break my training,'

'I do not ask for that. I ask for nothing. Your destiny is yours. But when you look at the stars or see the birds, take the time to see and hear.'

Months passed, and the young man trained. Every full moon he saw a new bird and visited the old man. A year passed, and he was covered with bird tattoos, most he kept hidden under his clothes.

One night, when the two men were having tea together, the old man said, 'I have another secret for you.'

Akio bowed, saying, 'Thank you, Sensei.'

'Touch the tattoo, think of the bird and sing.'

Akio raised his hand to touch the first tattoo.

'Wait till you are on your own. Your experience must be pure. Take this – a book of Haiku. 'Read and think of what you feel.'

Akio bowed and found a flat rock between trees to sit on in the shade. He touched his tattoo and his mind filled with bird song. He sang to the stars, astonished to hear his voice. He sat under the stars, watching them and thinking of the song from the songbird tattoos. He touched another tattoo and again filled with song; he felt calm, but his heart beat faster; he sang to the stars, to the moon.

Every full moon he would come to sing in his chosen place on the rock, surrounded by soft green moss. On every third moon a peculiar thing happened – while he was singing, he felt his skin itch; the tattoos on his arms, on his chest seemed to be moving, first the birds trembled as if shaking off dust, and then they opened their beaks one by one. The bird tattoos stretched their wings, glided around his body, like colourful shadows in his skin. Akio felt a light flutter, a caress, as the birds moved. One flew from his chest to his waist and down to his leg, to settle on his left foot; another leapt from his shoulder up his neck to hover on his cheek; a third left his belly, rose up along the backbone, flew across the shoulders and settled on his forearm. One by one, the tattoo birds peeled from his skin, breathed in and filled out, stretched their wings, and rose into the sky. They flew to the top of the trees, to above the trees and sang.

Akio sat cross-legged on the rock, listened to the song and watched the birds flying, colourful shapes like living musical kites high above. He sat there all night as the birds played. Just before sunrise, they flew back to him one by one, stood on their tattoos and, as if absorbed by the skin, re-joined the tattoos that seemed brighter than before. The last bird settled, he rolled down his sleeves and ran to the old man's house between the trees.

The old man was sitting on the tatami mat, having tea, with two cups in front of him.

'You were expecting me?'

The old man smiled.

Akio excitedly told of the night before.

The old man listened, stroking his long wispy white beard.

'Did you know this would happen, Sensei?'

The old man opened his shirt and showed his tattoos on his wrinkled skin. 'My body will soon be a poor home for these birds. They can all be yours if you would do me the honour of accepting them. You are graced by the soul of the song-birds, treat them well.'

Akio bowed. 'The honour would be all mine.'

The old man took out a bundle wrapped in silk from behind his back. 'For you.'

Akio opened the bundle. There lay three books – one of the old man's hand-drawn birds, the second was *Hagakure – The Book of the Samurai,* and the last, a blank book. 'Yours to fill. What will be written is your choice.'

The next day Akio was training, leaping and arcing his sword as he glided through the air, landing silently, only a small cloud of dust rising near his feet. He looked up. Three Samurai on horses galloped towards him. Akio's eyes flickered briefly, and he leapt and turned again, sweeping his sword, and sheathed it as he landed. He bowed and looked at the three Samurai, now dismounted, their horses behind them. They stood in a line before him – shoulder to shoulder – In the middle stood the tallest, black hair tied back into a topknot, a grey silk kimono with an inlaid crest; his two swords, each with ornate woven handles, were sheathed. On left and right, stood two stockier Samurai, in battle armour made of leather and iron scales, lacquered helmet with upturned crescent moons. Each had a grimacing mask, one wooden and one metal, with slits for eyes.

The taller of the Samurai bowed, walked up to a nearby tree, tied a thin plank of wood to a string and dangled it from a branch. 'Pierce it with your sword.'

The young man drew his sword and lunged at the wood; the wood flew back, jerked on the rope, and swung around.

The Samurai did not say anything, just nodded.

The young man sat and contemplated the wood, how it swung, looked at his sword, stood up and drove his sword forward; this time it struck and stuck.

'There is hope for you,' said the Samurai, 'But the path to being a Samurai is not an easy one.'

'I train every day in the hope of catching your noble interest,' said Akio.

'People have spoken of you and you have our attention,' said the one with the wooden mask.

'People have also said that you are a bird man,' said the metal masked warrior pointing at the tattoo on the young man's arm. 'The way of the Samurai is pure allegiance. Will birds distract you in a fight?'

'They strengthen me,' said Akio, 'I learn how to use the air to move the body, how to leap and land in silence, how to twist and turn to avoid the claws and beak of enemies.'

'Show us your allegiance,' said the tall Samurai, nodding to the man with the wooden mask who stepped forward, holding out a bamboo cage that had been hidden behind his back. In it was a blue and green songbird with a red silk cord attached to its neck. He grabbed the bird, knotted the silk cord to a branch and threw the bird into the air. 'Prove your commitment to the way. Take your sword.'

Akio started to protest but looked at the immobile faces of the three Samurai. 'My story is to be written,' he said to himself. He raised his sword and approached the bird. It flew frantically at first, but as he concentrated on the bird, its flight calmed, and it seemed to hover in front of him for a split second.

Akio thrust his sword forward, watching the bird. He saw the terror in the bird's eyes; it gave a little cry, a beautiful note. His arms kept moving forward; his sword flashed towards the bird. Something inside Akio called to him. He closed his eyes and pulled back his sword. The song was gone, and Akio opened his eyes. He had stopped his sword but three feathers fell from the bird's chest, and three drops of blood. He ran forward to catch the bleeding bird; more feathers drifted to the ground.

The tall Samurai laughed. 'You are quick and have the skills to be a Samurai. However, you failed your test of allegiance. You are a bird man and not a Samurai.' He pushed the bamboo cage with his foot towards Akio. 'Keep the bird.' The three turned as one and left without looking back.

Akio, the wounded bird in his hands, fell to his knees. He tried not to cry. The blood from the bird dripped into the dust. He felt a pain in his stomach, and he looked under his shirt. One of the bird tattoos had changed – it now had a thin streak of blood from its chest and hurt.

Akio got up, untied the bird and went into the forest to the old man's home.

He found the old man waiting for him.

'I have been a fool, Sensei,' he said, showing the wounded bird. 'Can you help?'

'You have shown great courage to fight off the destiny of your dreams. You have chosen well. Together we will heal this bird; then I will teach you more of the forest, and you can write your own path.

Akio touched his side and showed the bleeding tattoo to the old man.

'It will bleed to remind you of the choice you made and the choice you almost made,' said the old man. 'But the bird will still sing and fly.'

Young Akio looked at the wounded bird and said, 'I have dishonoured your trust.'

'You stood up to one destiny and have chosen the open path. You stood up to three Samurai and showed the soul to be stronger than steel. Many would have killed the bird and realised only too late, or even never, the choice they were facing. You do me a very great honour,' said the old man, bowing. He then bared his side – showing a tattoo of a bird. It was all black and still. A black tattoo among colourful birds.

The Voyager's Ode against the Sirens

You tempt me with your song
But I hear the melodies of robins and blue jays
You tempt me with your beauty
But I think of snow leopards and sunrise

You offer me fame and glory
And I remember my love's look
You offer me riches beyond my dreams
But they reek of hollow dreams for empty men

You beckon me with tales of old
With music that has seen the stars
That with you I may weave words and notes like masters
But I know the truest spring lies within me

You shout that I will wither and wilt
That my mind will slow and my wit will dull
My eyes will cloud and all will be mist
You whisper—with me you can live forever

I laugh at your lies and your empty promises,
Your tarnished temptations that seek to tether me to you
You say that I can fly free as a bird
But I know that a bird with a heart of rock can only fall

You lay out banquets before me
With flowers, sweet fruit, and scented dishes
With clearest waters, and rich wines to quench my thirst

But I see the truth – it is your hunger that you seek to sate

You whisper that I should not be a fool
Live like a lion and a king, and you hold out a sceptre and crown
You offer me the rolling lands, the seas and sky
But what use is all that, if I hand you my soul

Seek another with your words and wiles I say
I will sail far from thee.
You will not have my flesh nor my spirit
Eat of the rocks and drink of the sea

You are Sirens pretending to be gods and angels
Sirens standing on cold barren rocks
Wetted by storms and salty seas, offering empty treasures
But you seek only the warm flesh of fools

May the rains slake your thirst
The sun warm your cold hearts
The winds fill your lungs
And the fruits of the earth abate your hunger

For I will sail far from thee

Simon Boylan

May 2015

Romantic Ireland's back again, it's risen bleary from the grave.
Rumours of its demise were greatly exaggerated
What a strange thing to have to vote on love,
As though it was something that could be legislated

But, though surreal, it has given us hope
That the long shadow cast by a pope
Has finally been chased from our shores
To smother our souls never more.

Because it's time for something new
Something real and something true.
People who imagine each other
Complexly rather than as class clones,
Not just a gender or a race.
To be judged by their voice, their face.
A land of honest and warm
People here at peace
With themselves and each other
In this exposed place.

Maybe it's too late.
Maybe our days are numbered

Until the climate changes and it sucks us under
The sea at last returned.
But at least we did this one good thing
This overdue unburdening

Yes.
That glorious word yes
The affirmation yes
A lover yearns to hear it yes
We are
Together yes

I want our tortured forbears to see this land renewed.
I want those raped by priests to see a better view
Of their country before they pass.
I want those small bodies in the churchyard to be the last.

Oppressive Ireland's dead and gone, it's with the children in the grave,
Buried without names behind the workhouse.
It's a long road and a hard road but it begins with a single step.
A new way of living starts with a single yes.

Lida Papasokrati

First Date

Restaurant
First date
Shy smiles first
Then laughs, tingling hands
Mascara in the ladies' room
Didn't finish the food
Too busy talking
Best part:
Possibilities

Barbara Koethe

The Meal

-Hungry-
We walk.
We kneel down,
Open the basket.
On the blanket we picnic.
Tasty bites and nips
We get up
Walk off

Together

A boat on the sea
It moves gently with the waves
The wind's picking up
Pushes, curves and curls the waves
Darling, dance and drown with me!

Routine

Grapes she eats – fifteen –
She washes them till they are clean.
In the salad spinner they twirl times fifteen
Dizzy they are, but she is keen
On her daily lunch at twelve fifteen.

Yin-Yang

A new bicycle with a missing front wheel?
A lonely skip over a terracotta-shard on a beach in spring?
Sour milk flaking in a cup of fresh tea?
A dream orange with rust?
A tear falling off a false eyelash?
A sunbeam behind the rain?
A wedding ring hiding in a purse?
A wrinkled hand on a nipple?
Happiness with a runny nose?
A hole in the wall around our hearts?
A golden tooth on a pub floor?
Could be worse, ey?

Dead Weight

Can a van be on top of a boat?
A canoe on top of a van?
A bicycle on top of a canoe?
Yes they can!
                But the bicycle would not ride

The canoe would not swim
The van would not drive
And the boat would sink.

Can I be on top of you?
Yes, I can!

But I could not dance
And you could not see the colours of the sky
And our freedom was yesterday.

Can you be on top of me?
Yes, you can!

But you could not paint
And I could not breathe the air that I need
And we would stumble and finally fall.

Claire Davenport

The Last Student (Chapter One)

27 April 2015

Only now and again, struck by the absurdity of our
occupations, we grope after our lost consciousness and feel
somehow that somewhere out beyond is our real
destination, that somewhere out there a feast is
proceeding, that a cover is laid for us and dishes served,
that though we are absent the master calls a toast to us and
sends messengers to find us.

—*The Gentle Art of Tramping,* Stephen Graham

Women walked with yoga mats, their faces the cowardice
of the institutionalised, Europe or some such concrete blob
around the city. A bearded dwarf skimmed by them,
waddling hips brushing their calves. Arab men in pairs and
dark round bomber jackets gesticulated to each other in
guttural songs like typewriters in a Disney film. Pock marked
women poured into knee-highs pontificated, fags in hand,
mincing at passers-by.

Janis nestled the saddle of her bike under her pelvis as
the two took off in communion down hills to her reporting
job. The streets before her flattened beyond Mont des Arts
and she began pedalling wildly. The traffic was heavy so she
got creative or so she thought, keeping one eye on the
edges of cars and pavements and the other on traffic cops.

One-way streets interfered so she hit alleys and then before her the new tunnel, almost black but for a speck of amber. She started down it, steadfast, on a low gear but to her astonishment saw a lorry careering towards her. The driver's head jolted over the dashboard, registering Janis, as one hand plunged into the horn. She jumped off the bike and sharply tugged it like a large dead body back fifty metres to the tunnel's mouth, vaulting with it over a low grey boundary at the side of the road. The lorry sped past, hooting and her yellow supermarket bike flew and bounced in spite of its heavy cheap frame. An espresso shot delivered intravenously, she thought, as she ambled to work, her bike now disobediently veering left and right next to her.

This was how Janis learned that the new tunnel was one-way, trivia she looked forward to sharing with her colleagues who had a taste for small dramas between the coffees that drowned erstwhile dreams of reports in troubled neighbourhoods with troubled people. Brussels was good at pretending to be troubled, as were they.

"Can everybody please shut up? I cannot hear myself think." Penny, her colleague, could be heard imploring. Colleagues threw their eyes to heaven, but nobody ever snipped back. And not one inch of their journalistic pathos or integrity or any other grandiose self-ascribed qualities these gatekeepers of information mythically possessed eked out of them the courage to stand up to the powers above them, 'that pay-cutting shower of millionaires.' "Did you know so-and-so gets 3.8 million a year?" one would say over a beer that at one point of the evening inevitably became a self-help group over the uppers and how they treat the lowers. And so they went on, grumbling inwardly, doing, pouring outrage into stories over new gizmos and banks and laws regulating the consumerism of the middle class.

It was a Thursday and Janis got in at six that morning to answer last night's mails and skim the papers for news. The morning duty was a coming of age, something she had evaded gladly, but now her name stood on the roster. Most, including Janis, made their way to the morning shift dreading all the global desks of her company, Rubicon, weighing in with curt emails about this or that "missed story" from the night before. Her editor, Jason, a man of few words and many hushed phone calls breezed in to commence the days' desk banging and heavy typing that gave him an air of unburied memories, true or not. He had been in Iraq, people around the office whispered.

"Everything ok?" he asked that morning loitering unusually at her desk. "Yes," she offered. He asked her if she had a minute, the dissonance between the question and his intentions palpable. And without asking her to follow him or making declarations about the weather, he spun on his heels and marched to a room in the back of the office. She had never been there before. He asked her to sit at a small table where a childlike blonde's thin fingers slid a sheet of paper in front of her. "Janis, you know we have had to make cutbacks," Jason said, for once shaking as he spoke. "Well, this is going to come as a shock. We have to let you go."

Janis could not remember well their faces after those words or the other words that were exchanged thereafter. There was something about severance. Would she sign now? No. Sooner than later was better, they pleaded. OK. She remembers how the pointy-featured blonde woman curled her eyebrows upwards. Feigned sympathy. How she conceded that it would be hard. Eyebrows again. That they would help. An awkward nightingale, her hand touched Janis's arm reluctantly acting out a HR training exercise.

Janis saw the heron at the lake, the one she saw on her Sunday runs, tall and blinking into the air. "So this is your last day. You can work a full day or leave now, as you wish," was the last thing the man said to her. And so she walked and left it all there. The papers, the contacts, the emails, the tea stains, the job, a little installation she could just abandon like a Tracy Emin bed. She spilled out onto the street and her legs started homewards but took a sharp turn into a Congolese bar.

"J'ai perdu mon boulot," she said to the attractive tall African waitress whose tilted eyes were observing Janis standing at the bar at 11am, their only customer. The woman poured a beer, shunning payment. Janis felt like she had oil clogging her brain, preventing the synapses from linking. Her life revolved around getting here, she thought, around believing that great things happen in offices where superior men and women sit and teach underlings the ways of the world. Her family cherished the working men and women of the world. What would everyone think now, she thought time and again, a bird crashing into a window pane it could not see.

The image of a bike came back to her. In need of loneliness Janis took her beer outside and lit up. She texted and emailed everyone she knew and revelled in their shock. What? WTF? Oh my god, where are you? And so the girl whose life had been crafted in an image acceptable to everybody else was now telling them it had all come undone. They were all sorry, of course.

*

Decay. She shut the window. It had only been open five minutes. Blocked drain keeping last week's shower water afloat. Attracting flies. Kitchen sink full of dishes. Pyjamas taking on smell of sweat. Afternoon naps permissible. Looking out windows. Smoking out windows. Watching birds. Envying birds. Staring at the terrace banister and then the distance down to the ground. Would that kill you? Friends on idiotbook.com posting pictures, articles. Living lives outwardly. Wittily, sometimes. Nothing to add. Eating remnants of food. Eating from tins. How much tea can one person drink in a day? One or two missed calls. Why is talking so important? Mother keeps herself awake at night worrying. Daughter worrying for worrying mother. Mother and Granddad keep asking: Have you looked at any jobs? Daughter keeps saying: I don't think I want a job right now. Daughter must repeat herself. Daughter is tired.

*

It was Wednesday. Janis sat in one of Brussels' many hipster cafes perusing new career paths. She was on the Gs. Geologist. Gynaecologist. Gymnast. Gin events manager. The latter seemed promising. The waitress was the owner's grumpy daughter, all short-haired and pixie-faced and angry. When orders seemed to dissipate she cranked up the music until someone mustered the courage to ask her to turn it down. Her time was divided between raising an imperious chin to accept an order, scanning iTunes for the next track and checking out people on Facebook. What would Chomsky say about Facebook, Janis wondered. Would he recall Orwell and say that Facebook was made because too much gin would run up health costs? Or was that film right, some boy who went to a big school plagued by hierarchy wanted to know which girls he could screw and now we were all on it either doing the same or spouting crap. 'Who wants to march against the no public drinking ban', one of Janis's 453 Facebook friends asked in a post. It occurred to her, she had spent a large part of the last ten years drinking in public.

At the counter a little girl sucked her lips and stared over at the waitress. Janis saw herself. Twelve. Freshly-jutting hips rested against the old wood of a bar in a café in Kontich. It was her new favourite thing, to feel her hips against things. When she got home after school, she would change out of her boring school clothes into her Levis and walk around the town with one hand on one hip and an arched back to show the growth of two new lumps. Maral her Iranian friend once asked if she could touch them and she did, with one finger like a child at a dead cat on the road. That night she wore her mother's grey, baggy sweater to hide the lumps from Granddad who from time to time said strange things like "don't leave dents in that jumper." The barman was triumphantly pouring dark red Chimay into big glasses. He winked at her. It was one of the rare times she could join Lynn, her mother, when she collected Granddad "from the cafe."

Granddad or Wim or Wimke paraded daughter and granddaughter to local men. "And this is my schatje, my Janis. Jaja. Like Janis Joplin. She's a bit shy but we are working on it." The men patted her shoulder. Janis turned from their loud voices to her own world, knocking her hips against the bar, sucking, observing.

Now 30, Janis and her dents and her hips needed a sign. The sullen waitress threw down two coffees on a table that seemed to be hosting a job interview. A burly man widening the seams of his suit asked an angel-faced young girl about the level of her "Inglish." The girl clasped her hands mildly over straight and together knees and said: "Yes I sink it is gud." Then she took a deep breath with her large chest and said no more, gazing shyly at the table. The man said, "Well zis is a point of attention, hmm?" Then he asked her where she saw herself in five years and she shrugged meekly, twisted her lips, ummed and awed and said, "As a HR manager in a large or maybe medium sized company."

She bit down hard on her lower lip as she feigned the worldliness she probably otherwise possessed, and shakily lifted her coffee cup. Janis felt herself wishing she could go over to the table and encourage her to lift her shoulders and flap her hands mid-talking and smile. But she continued doe-eyed and hunched, clamping one lip over the other as though the inside of her mouth was busy washing itself. The waitress turned up the music. "Hey lady luck is on your side, hey lady let's go out tonight." Janis asked for the bill and made her way to the unemployment office where she had an appointment. The job interview had now turned into a lecture: "My Inglish is not good either but I try."

The teacher or whatever he was at the employment office looked like a member of the BeeGees with green flares and a brick red and orange jumper.

He started with some general questions like, what do you think we are here for? And how can you help yourself? Some of the goodies at the front kept answering. Oompaloompas in a song: You are here to help us and we should apply to as many jobs as possible. There were quite a few in the back row, there were just five rows, who were older than the hipster teacher and fired questions like, "Will the next government honour our social welfare payments" and "when you merge with the other company what will that do to us." Janis tuned in and out.

"I am not a politician" the hipster said aghast and, "Yes we arrh merrhging with anotherrh company and I have no idea what will happen afterrh that. I don't have a crrhystal ball." An older man maybe around forty years old in the fifth row was unhappy with these answers. "You cannot tell us to be proactive without knowing if we will still have your support." There were nods around the room. Janis was already tired. She never had a good sense of what money was. It appeared, sometimes it disappeared and so she ate bread and sweetcorn for a while. The session had now turned into a political discussion. The Flemish nationalists want to take away our welfare, an Arab man said. The hipster managed to close off the debate by saying the longer it took the more time he would need for his session. And so he droned on about discounts on public transport, training, but in the end it is all up to you to apply yourself. Sitting there she wondered what had compelled this ABBAman to work here.

At her flat that evening a dusky red sky spilled into the living room as she mistakenly relayed the day to Mark her ex-boyfriend who wrong-footed Janis with a sympathy call. Mark was a Christian Democrat public servant who loved his job and never cut his toenails. She felt unworthy in his presence now, this trust-funded bohemian. "You can tell someone is really rich when they don't know how to dress," her mother said when she first met him and Janis quietly seethed at her truisms.

"Yeah, well you can tell that those people have no intention to work if all they want to know is will the new government stop their payments?" Mark ranted, searing through Janis with a large spear who suddenly found herself choked up about benefit claimants.

"What? Mark they would not show up if that were the case."

"They show up because they are afraid they won't get their payments."

"That's simply not true Mark. The Belgian state does nothing to follow up on the unemployed."

"Oh c'mon stop blaming us!"

And there it was, Janis and Mark and the reason they were no longer together. It had all ended over lentils in the end. He planned to make her a lentil curry but threw the ingredients in the bin once he learned that she ate beans for lunch. "They are part of the same food group," he shouted and she packed a bag and left.

A gentle rain lilted to the pavement and Janis excused herself to go out and sulk. As the rain quickened suddenly it hid the water now streaming from her eyes. The charm of some small green exotic birds she watched cawing and shivering at the base of a tree in the park ebbed and flowed. Nevertheless, they were green, they were moving, they were not ex-boyfriends and they were not at a job interview. So she watched them for over an hour, one by one flapping behind another as though they were alternating to knead an invisible bit of bread dough.

*

"What...did you do? What did you do for me? I do everything," a woman could be heard commanding over the music that swept in and out her bedroom window as Janis lay ensconced in her smoky duvet, her hair still wringing wet.

"Without men there is nothing, you know that you stupid woman," a man said barely pausing for breath. The woman could be heard cackling, mocking and returned:

"Without me, you would have nothing. Without my business! I did everything."

"Eh you cut hair. What you talking about business for? That's not business."

Children's feet chomped pebbles in a game of chase. The argument grew louder and others continued talking and laughing in concurrent conversations regardless. Janis closed the door, had a shower, opened a bottle of wine and took her book downstairs to the bedroom where next door's party lightened and washed away.

At 3am she awoke abruptly from a dream she couldn't remember save the vague image of a bike and a road. She had left her bedside light on and flicked it off, turning sideways to face the garden, nuzzling further into her duvet. Her bed lay next to a floor-to-ceiling window that stretched the entire outer wall of the room. Her eyes clamped shut again, but a flickering light persisted either in or outside her eyelids. She would need courage to open her eyes now for bad things came in threes, and with the break up and the layoff, this could very well be it, number three, her murder, she thought. So she peeled open one eye slowly to discover a bright rectangular box of light hovering on the right garden wall. Pebbles could be heard crunching underfoot and Janis felt her neck tense and thicken with pulsating veins. She pulled the duvet up around her face, then down again to hear. Crunch. Crunch. The sound was close. Her eyes and veins widened again to the appearance of a shadow of a hand in the box of light, and a leg and then a whole 8-foot apparition of a tiptoeing figure. And then its six-feet source, a man wearing what could have been a red or pink t-shirt seemed to worm through a window next to her bedroom. She catapulted into an upright position, frozen, scanned her room for doors, but all she saw was the bathroom on the other side of the room. She heard doors closing. A television began to blare. Janis grabbed the wine bottle, downing the glassful left to knock herself out. It did.

Larisa Doctorow Zalesova

Bali Rendez-vous

BALI- A SENTIMENTAL JOURNEY

For many years my father had been telling me, 'You should go to Bali. It is so beautiful'. His words sounded reproaching, but we young, carefree and having moved to Europe from New York, craved to see European countries, Paris, London, Madrid...

By profession he was a geographer and later in his life became a diplomat. Indonesia was his last post and produced a very strong impression. Coming from Russia with its severe winters, gloom and cold of several months, he found himself in the tropics. It must have been shocking. As long as he lived, he never forgot Indonesia. He brought back tons of films, photos of indigene dances, local festivals and parades and after his return, for years he lectured about that beautiful country with rich culture. In those days very few Russians had the opportunity to travel and his lectures gathered full halls.

My parents have also brought back a number of carved wooden sculptures and one painting. It depicted female figures at the background of green lush bushes. My father put it on the wall in the living room. He died under it years later.

Finally the moment to go to Bali has arrived. But my father is not here anymore and I can't share with him my impressions.

The flight lasted for many hours, the longest leg was between Frankfurt and Singapore, it also was the hardest. Sitting for 12 hours in the economy narrow seats was not a pleasure. But the reward was the airport itself.

Entering NAME the airport, my husband looked at hundreds of flowering bushes and orchids and mumbled, 'Typical Chinese decoration. They love artificial flowers'.

I objected,' They seem to me real'. He touched one and exclaimed,' They are real!'

The central part of the arrival hall was taken by flowering islets, where wooden benches and tables were set amidst orchid plants and exotic trees, resembling a botanical garden. Next to them there were small ponds with bright red and white fish splashing.

By local time it was close to midnight, so we could not see much on the way from the airport to our hotel.

Our first week was spent in Benoa Novotel. Novotel sounds middle, middle, but this one is four stars. It is a genuine resort set on a sea shore in a tropical garden. We walked to our chalet along trails lit by vases with flowers lit inside. The atmosphere was magic. Similar lights would be accompanying us nightly in four different locations on the island. It was amazingly warm, around 27 degrees. Looking out at the starry sky, I could not find the Dipper or the North Star which confirmed my expectations that I have really crossed the equator. Reading in the books that the travelers doing so are welcome by the Neptune, I was disappointed that on our flight nobody sprinkled us with sea water. Probably, my expectations fell out of fashion a long time ago. Needless to say, I woke up in the middle of the night. It will take time for the body to change its inner clock. It was very quiet as if we had no neighbors. In front of the chalet there was a garden and chalets were separated by walls and green shrubs, which provided a complete privacy.

Upon our arrival late at night we hardly paid attention to the lobby of our hotel, which it is worth mentioning. A huge construction in local wood with very high ceilings emphasized the traditional Balinese architectural style. Thick grass-thatched roof covered the all -timber lobby area, protected by bamboo curtains from rain or wind. There were no walls. The whole area was open to the stars, birds chirping and the aroma of plumeria trees blooming the whole year round. This tree covered with white or yellowish flowers grows everywhere. Its flowers' fragrance resemble our jasmine, the flowers are rather hardy and are widely used for decorating tables, offerings, sculptures. Every waiter on the island has a plumeria flower behind his ear.

Next day, just after six in the morning, we went for a quick swim. The choice was between the pool and the sea. Both were attractive. Black sand beach was licked by silky waves, swimming pools looked like natural lakes decorated with stone sculptures and flowering shrubs. The whole complex is constructed like a low-rise Balinese village. In the tropics the day ends early, by seven p.m. the night falls briskly like a curtain in a theatre.

Gradually I started looking at Bali through my father's eyes. He was enchanted by luxuriant nature, the climate, close bonds of people with nature. In this remote from Europe part of the world one can't help but experience the overwhelming sensation how small is the place in the world occupied by Europe.

We have entered a different universe and had one month to discover it. After two breakfasts with generous choice of local fruit I could not only recognize them, but also learn the names. Salak- crocodile skin fruit, rambutan- hairy fruit covered with soft red hair, dragon fruit with intense crimson red flesh – these were a novelty, to them I will add small milky bananas, pineapples, mangos and oranges. It was not Europeans who name the island Paradise, it was the Balinese. Bali has plenty of water, fruit, vegetables in abundance, including rice, forests and a great climate.

Among the trees the most veneered and admired is Banyan tree, half of branches grow up and half down , turning into additional roots and supporting the tree, spreading for many meters. They call it the eternal tree. If the tree is cut, the roots push shoots further away from the cut trunk. But the Balinese don't cut them. In one village Banyan tree got so big that impeded the traffic. The local commune cut some of the supporting roots and freed the street for through traffic.

We went to Bali at the beginning of January to escape Belgian rains and gloom. A week before we were supposed to leave, we leant that January in Bali is a part of rainy season and it rains daily. It was too late to cancel the trip, so we decided to go and face rainy days. It has turned out that it was just right, because in rainy season it is not so hot, and it does not rain daily. The rains are short, and in the next several minutes everything dries out.

Tourist season in Bali is in close relation with the Australian school calendar. In 2013 25% of tourists came from Australia. In our Novotel we really have seen the world at our doorstep. For about five days there was a tribe of Lebanese from Australia who took a good chunk of the facility. 53 of them in all, maybe one third consisting of babies aged 1 to 3, and another third of grannies in their head to toe wraps. In the late afternoon they settled near the pool and the old ladies brought in their water pipes. After they departed, their place was taken by a flock of young and affluent looking Chinese, then came the usual complement of Australians and Japanese. Since 2003 the Russians come to Bali regularly. When our plane was landing, next to it there was a Russian plane from Novosibirsk. I can imagine their bewilderment experiencing plus 31 degrees instead of minus 25.

After one week in Benoa we moved to Ubud, the artistic capital of the island. I can tell frankly, if we have not seen Ubud, Bali experience would turn into another beach resort vacation for which you don't need to travel for 20 hours. The Canary Islands or Morocco serve Europeans well as the winter holiday beach destination, but Ubud is worth the trip.

Ubud has the population of 48 000 people, but is famous throughout Indonesia as a special place. Its fame began in the 17th century well before the Europeans took a keen interest in its economic possibilities. It is set amidst tropical forests along the valleys of two rivers and surrounded by rice paddies. At the background one can see the mountain ridge with two active volcanoes.

To get to our luxurious hotel Komaneka, we traveled along the main road, then turned to a smaller road passing through the village, where the farmers' houses were lodged behind thick shrubs and banana trees. Strong smell of animals, chickens pecking along the road and cow mooing made me wonder, whether it was possible to have a five stars hotel in such a place. To enhance my doubts, our taxi stopped at a small wooden pavilion, in front of which I spotted a small parking, filled in with mopeds. The rain was pouring. The driver opened a huge umbrella above my head and showed the way to the reception. As the reception a woman explained to us that during wet season in Ubud it rains daily from 14 to 16. All the activities are scheduled accordingly. To get to our chalet we waited till the rain subsided.

We had a bedroom, combined with a living room and a dining room, equally big bathroom, in the middle of which a huge stone bath cut from a piece of lava occupied the centre of the room opened to a small garden with a swimming pool. The canapé of white flowers hanging from a tree served as a shield against the sun. There was no wind and the palm branches stood still on the background of the sky like silhouettes in the theatre of the shadows.

The place of thousand temples, all in brick of purple Pompei colors, of 100 restaurants, of three museums and numerous art galleries and stone carving workshops, Ubud exists since the ninth century. A man from India came to spread Hinduism and taught the locals agriculture. People from Java running from Moslems moved here. Thanks to that man Balinese Hinduism exists here. This is the place where traditional medicine is strong, healers are held in high esteem, where still there live royal families and their descendants. Here there are casts, but their meaning and influence weakens. For example, the governor of the island comes from the low cast, from the family of farmers.

The week spent in Komaneka Tanggayuda hotel was heaven itself.

The boutique hotel with just 37 lodgings on the outskirts of the town is set in a vast piece of tropical forest. When we reserved the hotel, we had no idea that the philosophy of the owners was so close to what we love. They are second generation art collectors. The family founded one of three art museums in the town and they have filled their resort with artifacts and sculptures in wood and stone, and period furniture. A fine aesthetic sensibility is seen in everything, including the oil lamps on short poles that are set up each evening along pathways and taken down in the morning, the floral offerings to the shrines all around the territory that the girls prepare daily and invite you to participate in. The complex is cheek and jowl with the native settlement of rice farmers who provide most of the staff. When you walk out in the morning and cross the local road, walking past scurrying free range chickens and lazy dogs, and busy farm hands all of whom smile and greet you in English, in 10 minutes you reach the rice paddies which are punctuated in the distance by coconut palms and come up occasionally to the very substantial masonry house compounds of farmer-owners.

On the other side, the hotel complex faces a river gorge and rain forest or terraced rice paddies. That is what you see over the edge of the two infinity pools. You have to be mad to leave this compound once you are installed. And yet most guests leave that magic place for shopping in town or to see Balinese fire dancing at a temple at night or to ride elephants. We stayed put in our villa, enjoyed the view from each corner of the house, the swimming pool and the garden and never felt tired. Our villa measured 900 square feet, had a walled in garden on one side and a walled in plunge pool and lounge area on the other side. These were the most luxurious lodgings we have ever rented, though the price was less than our Midtown Marriott when we were in NY last September. Sheer elegance throughout plus high service levels in the open air dining with knockout views of the river valley in the foreground and volcanic mountains in the distance. In the evening before sunset further romantic touches were added by rising mist from the valley.

Tree frogs quacking in complaint at the gamelan players on the deck level where we retired after having our dinners provided late evening entertainment.

The most traditional aspect of Balinese architecture which the new international designers try to follow is inside-outside, meaning bathrooms that are open to the air, living rooms with just bamboo venetian blind walls, in effect leaving bedrooms as fully insulated and air-conditioned and the very high, cathedral ceilings – all with effect to aerate and prevent build-up of humidity and mustiness.

Rice fields with their emerald green young sprouts are everywhere, they alternate with dirty looking fields, ready for planting. The buffalos walk by. Dividing the fields there are the canals where water babbles. They exist since the 9th century and local communities control the influx of water and its distribution.

Along the road on both sides there are thousands of carved stone figures of deities, of animals, some are huge. They are intended for private temples. People have temples inside their courtyards, behind fences. In any hotel there are temples, for which mesaiban-the offerings are provided fresh every day, set on small squares of banana leaves.

UBUD is called art village. Many artists lived and worked there and more live and work now. Some of them are rice farmers in the morning and painters in the afternoon. There are innumerable art galleries set on both sides of the main street. I asked someone, whether they sell their art, the person replied, that if they don't sell, they would not exhibit their paintings and would not be there. The European artists started coming here in the 1920-1930s and still this trend continues.

The most famous was Walter Spies. Everyone in Ubud knows this name. He set up a studio and taught the Ududians to paint, now the house where he lived is a museum. His works and the works of other Europeans and Indonesians are exhibited in Ubud. His fate is tragic.

When the Second World War broke out, he was arrested and interned because he was a German citizen. He was sent by the Dutch with other interned Germans to Sumatra and from there to Ceylon. On the way the ship was bombed by the Japanese and the Dutch saved their nationals and let others drown. It was in 1942.

Bali History

Dutch interest in Bali began only during-after the Napoleonic Wars, when Holland was occupied by the French, when its Indies colonies were taken by the British. Prior to that Dutch interaction going back to the late 16th century, was limited to brief ship visits and desultory trade. Starting in the 1830s the growing ship traffic between Singapore and Australia made Bali, with its surfeit of rice and other commodities, an important provisioning point. The Dutch colonial sovereignty began to be introduced by force in the late 1840s with a succession of military expeditions that imposed treaty conditions on the northern radjas. The process reached its culmination in the 1906-08 period when the southern radjas also succumbed. But the bloody self-sacrifice of the southern courts in which thousands killed themselves in front of the Dutch troops had reverberations in Holland and Europe, and the Dutch responded with an ethical policy under which they would not interfere with the culture and traditions of the Balinese, while the Balinese royalty would not intervene in local administration, which was overseen directly by Dutch Controllers. Thus Bali was spared the fate of other Indonesian territories and not turned into a plantation of rubber plants.

Since 1949 Bali like the rest of Indonesia is independent.

Riga 2014 –European Capital of Culture

Latvia may be a small Baltic state with a total population under two million, but it has produced a remarkable amount of world class art, theater, music and architecture, with outstanding performers who go out into the world. A great deal of those riches and a bit more than one-third of the population are concentrated in the capital, Riga, and in nearby locations to the north and south, so you can scoop up a lot of pleasurable experiences in a four or five day visit while relying on public transportation.

This year the effort of getting there is all the more worthwhile since Riga bears the title of Cultural Capital of Europe, and it has mobilized its resources, presenting to visitors and to the home side the best of the best from among numerous events and sites.

I came to Riga at a good moment. The end of April was sunny with temperatures in the 20s in daytime, providing real encouragement to get around town on foot and savor the street scene. Of course, since Riga is set in the North of Europe, weather is variable. The best time to visit is late spring and the summer months.

In any case, during my visit there were also formal indoors venues like the ballet evenings at the Riga Opera house, a presentation of a new oratorio by one of the leading Latvian composers at the Cathedral, an art exhibition entitled 'Art Days 2014. Dialogue', where works by the leading Latvian painter Vija Celmina, now living in New York, were presented. Events of this type will be available straight through to the year's end.

To get a brief orientation and learn about Riga 2014 events, visitors can stop by the 2014 Culture Chalet in the Esplanade Park which operates from May to the beginning of October. Coffee and other refreshments are available. There is live music at fixed times. The Chalet is run by the city administration as a meeting place open to all.

At the opening of the Chalet on 29 April, there was music and an inviting dance floor, very much in line with Latvian tradition, which reserves the day for dancing and singing around the city in schools, offices and green. Some professionals were there to break the ice and help folks get started. We managed to do a few dance steps as well.

Riga was always an important city going back to its two centuries as part of the Russian empire, when it was the third largest after Moscow and St Petersburg. Before that it was long a member of the Hanseatic League, connected with merchant cities stretching from Bruges in Flanders (now Belgium) in the West to Novgorod the Great in the

East. Back then it was the principal port on the Baltic Sea. And even today the port of Riga is an essential part of the city life, serving both freight vessels and passenger ships operating in the Baltic region. Riverside architecture reflects these activities, with warehouses, railway links and maritime symbols on the facades of the buildings

The skyline of the city is shaped by the domes and spires of its churches. The main Cathedral, now Protestant, dates from the 13th century and is a key landmark, set within a five minute walk from of the wide Daugava (Dvina) river and not far from the Riga bay. In the area adjoining Esplanade, there is an Orthodox cathedral, built in the early 1890s, which is also magnificent and worth a visit.

The city has an historic center, Old Riga, where you can wander the narrow and meandering medieval streets and small squares. And there is a newer part dating from the 19th century, which is distinguished by wide, tree-lined avenues passing between imposing Jugendstil period buildings. Riga is proud to claim the largest number of such buildings in Europe and their scale is interesting, two or more stories higher than in that other capital of Art Nouveau, Brussels. There are also numerous parks which make the city among the greenest in Europe.

Steep taxes on driving into the downtown zone work as an effective discouragement, so that the air in Riga is remarkably less polluted than in other European capitals. Frequent winds coming off the Baltic Sea also help. Both factors make it very pleasurable to stroll along Riga streets.

The sea has given Latvia one of its most famous treasures – sunny amber. Riga is the city of amber. Starting around 35,000 years ago, Baltic amber, the 'gold of the north,' travelled overland, southwards to the

Mediterranean. Amber's journey did not stop there: examples have been discovered in Tutankhamun's tomb and other Egyptian cities, in India and elsewhere. Now the city has three different exhibitions featuring amber and its influence from the point of view of European cultural contacts, its mythology and folklore. At the Museum of the History of Medicine, visitors can see an amber dress, borrowed for this temporary exhibition from a private collector, and a unique 2 kg piece which everyone can touch.

The American painter of Latvian origin Vija Celmina, whose works are an embodiment of modern trends in the arts, is showing off 50 works at the Riga Bourse Museum. The exhibition is considered one of the major Riga 2014 events. The paintings, etchings and sculptures on display embrace the 50 years from 1964 to 2014 and demonstrate her various techniques. In the 1960s the artist was fascinated by the ever changing surface of the ocean, in 1970s- by the depth and metaphysical loneliness of the desert and the sky. In her art one can find the influence or traces of pop-art, conceptualism, photorealism, which combined to create her unique universe filled with Buddhist calm. Now the Latvian National museum of Art possesses nine of her works including 'America,' an aquatint of 2010.

Local artists exhibit their wares in the numerous galleries around the city, as well as in private homes. Among them an exciting opening took place last week in the Gallery of Artists' Union of Latvia. Its title speaks for itself: "Art Days 2014. Dialogue." Here you can see works by more than 80 visual arts professionals and art students from the whole country, giving you a comprehensive picture of the direction young artists follow now. Personal expression, personal feelings, attitudes to the political situation in the neighboring countries all make it honest and worth seeing.

Music, classic and modern, follows strong traditions in Latvia. In the Soviet days many outstanding musicians and ballet dancers were educated here. The performers of world renown include violinists Gidon Kremer and Philippe Hirshhorn, cellist Misha Maisky, the dancers Michail Baryshnikov and Alexander Godunov.

The Riga opera house was the first in the Soviet Union where Richard Wagner's operas were performed in the original German language. Close to the Dome square, an old building bears a memorial plaque indicating this was the place where Wagner, Clara Schumann, Hector Berlioz and Franz Liszt performed. Wagner himself was the concertmaster of the Riga opera house for two years.

The evening of one act ballets 'Three Meetings' performed by the theater's own dance troupe proves the artistic tradition lives on. The ballets were staged by Denis Volpi, Mario Radacovsky and Bridget Breiner, Argentinian, Slovakian and American choreographers, and set to newly composed scores by our Latvian contemporaries.

Also in the past week, in the Riga cathedral on Dome Square, there was the world premiere of 'The Transcendental Oratory' by another modern Latvian composer Zigmar Liepins. The composer describes his work as 'the story of a mother's transcendental love.' It is devoted to the victims of the earthquake and tsunami in Japan. Rescue workers discovered a body of a woman under a collapsed building and beneath her a three month old boy, still alive, whom she was shielding with her body. The music by Zigmar Liepins is as touching, strong and moving as the story which inspired him. Latvian soprano Inga Slubovaska and world renowned tenor Alexandrs Antonenko were accompanied by the Latvian National Symphony Orchestra and State Academic Choir under the baton of Janis Liepins.

If the sampling of the high culture events overwhelms you and you want to rest in the great outdoors, just take a commuter train and head for Yurmala. In 30 minutes, you will find yourself among pine trees and sand dunes. The immaculate, fine white sand beach stretches for miles. The first stop where you can alight is Dzintary: that is where most of the restaurants are established and where Russian stars come to perform at a two week summer festival called the New Wave. We ate lunch in 'Sultans' (www.restoran-orient.lv) In spite of its name, the place's specialty is local sea food, including fresh sturgeon, raised nearby. There are also other Russian and Latvian classics. The meal was excellent, accentuated on this sunny day by local beer.

On the subject of food, Latvia is a rare example in Eastern Europe where chefs take pride offering local dishes and local products, preferably fresh and seasonable. In my five days, I ate in a number of restaurants in downtown Riga, in the palace restaurant of Rundale 80 km to the south and in the resort of Dzintary and never had a bad meal. Lunch can cost 6 euros in most places, while the lavish buffet lunch in the prestigious Radisson hotel is priced at 11 euros, you will agree this is reasonable. Dinner menus feature main dishes at 11 euros and under. Local beer is very good and an average is about 3 euros for a half-liter. A cup of quality coffee goes for 1.20 euros. Even though locals complain about prices rises of 20% ever since the euro was introduced at the start of the year, visitors will still find Latvia to be moderately priced by European standards. Fast food outlets are few and far between, sushi bars almost non-existent.

Any short visit to Riga should include the Jugendstil district, the new and much talked about KGB museum and the Occupation Museum. It also is very worthwhile making a day trip out to the palace of Anna I's favorite, Duke of Courland, Biron at Rundale.

The Jugendstil district which we mentioned in passing above, has been nicely restored in the twenty years since Latvia became independent. Most buildings were erected in the 1890s-1910s by investors as rental housing for the well-to-do. Facades are heavily decorated with stucco sculptural details, intricate balconies, turrets and stained glass windows. Among the most prolific architects of that period was Mikhail Eisenstein, the father of the famous Soviet film maker Sergei Eisenstein who designed 15 such houses. In one of them is the Art Nouveau Museum, which recreates an apartment of the early 20th century, including typical furnishings and a sampling of cookies handed out by an attendant in the kitchen.

Within short walking distance from this district there is the Occupation Museum (set in the former American Embassy) and the KGB building, generally known as the Corner House. The exhibition in the Occupation Museum opened in 1993 and is devoted to the painful years of the foreign occupation between 1940 and 1991, including the German occupation during the Second World War and the Soviet period that bracketed it. There are portraits of Hitler and Stalin set side by side.

In the newly opened KGB Museum, the basement and the first floor are ready to receive visitors. They are forewarned that the grim excursion 'is not advisable for children under 12.' Interrogation rooms, the execution room, cells where the arrested were kept and the gloomy courtyard tell us about how the building was used successively by the secret police of various regimes starting in 1935: first by the Latvian Ministry of State Security, in 1940 by KGB, then in 1941 by the Latvian puppet authorities installed by the Nazis and beginning in October 1944 again by KGB. Only in 2009 did the last officials of the State Latvian police leave the building (18 years after proclamation of the independence).

There are official attempts to downplay Russian influences in the history and art of Latvia, but that is not easy. The two palaces of Empress Anna's advisor Biron, together with their baroque gardens, one in Rundale and the other in Mitava, are the most famous cultural monuments of the country. They both were created in the 1730s by Bartolomeo Rastrelli, the Russianized Italian architect who built many palaces for the royal Russian family including The Winter Palace in St Petersburg. In spite of its age, the ravages of wars and various occupations over the centuries, the palace in Rundale has preserved many original features, including the oak parquet. In the garden behind the palace are some of the rose bushes which were first planted at the time the building was erected for its first owner, Ernst Johann Biron. Restoration of Rundale began immediately after the end of the Second World War and by the 1980s many halls were opened to visitors. Now this is a splendid museum which remains under the directorship of the same curator for nearly 40 years, Imants Lancmanis. Its major sponsor is the Russian-Latvian businessman Boris Teterev and his wife Inara. The museum has an excellent and modestly priced restaurant which should not be missed.

Shopping in Riga

Finally, a few words about shopping. Even though Riga has a good many international brands fashion boutiques, homegrown Latvian fashions remains a strong feature. Riga was always and remains remarkable for quality clothes made from wool, linen and cotton, often decorated with appliqués and embroidery. You see this in the selection on offer in Rigas Modes, one of the most famous fashion houses that has survived from Soviet times. Walking along Brivibas Street gives a good idea of the present day situation.

Jewelry shops offer amber in many different varieties of designs and price points for anyone seeking authentic Riga gifts.

Close to the main railways station, there is a Stockmann's department store and supermarket on the scale of their outlets in St Petersburg and Moscow, even if it is smaller than the Helsinki original. Next to it you'll find the Central Market, partly out on the street, partly in pavilions, offering a rich variety of fruits, vegetables, meats, smoked fish, dairy products and sausages that many visitors from Russia like to take home with them.

Мальта

Maltese Stories (Memories)

A real story with invented names

The retired Russian officer Nikolay Kravtsov came to Malta at the beginning of spring as the new director of the Russian Cultural Center, replacing his compatriot Alina Zorina.

The swift moving spring brought to life the island vegetation and every plant, tree or bush was returning to life proclaiming its happiness in multicolored flowers. Everything was blooming.

Having escaped the dark Moscow winter with snow storms, frost and ice, Nikolay was delighted. 'What a change! - He thought looking at mimosas swaying here and there under a delicate breeze.

When he was introduced to Alina, she turned out to be a plump woman of a certain age with dyed blond hair who spoke loudly and with convincing authority. After having spent three years on Malta, she and her husband were returning to Moscow.

Nikolay was an easy-going and well-disposed man, and people usually were disarmed by his round face, with a quick smile accompanied by merry sparkles in his blue eyes. His short grayish hair stubbornly rose at the top of his head and enhanced the pleasant impression.

Looking at him, one could be sure that the man appreciated a good joke, an anecdote, or an evening meal with the friends.

He was of an average height and effortlessly carried his slender, well-trained body.

Having spent all his life in Moscow at the Navy department of the Defense Ministry, he stayed there after retirement and was responsible for the logistics of sea routes for Russian ships.

When dealing with people, he adopted an instinctive manner, a mixture of ease and confidence which usually stimulated a similar friendliness in response. The same happened when he talked to Alina.

-Dear hostess, I am all ears. What advice would you give me? Admittedly, this is the first time in my life that I am in such a position. Everything here is new to me.

Alina's reply followed without delay:

-There is only one piece of advice. - She looked at him sharply - But you'd better listen to me attentively. Every week you should go to the Saint John Cathedral that is across the street and donate money for the repose of Sir Oliver Starki's soul.

-What!? – He stared at her.

-Here it is. And be generous, not tightfisted. I would also advise you to get a dog. We can't leave you our Rex.

-I am at a loss. What a recommendation! Looking through the budget sheets I don't remember such a column, or I have missed something?

-You are right, there is no budgetary item, and we paid for the masses from our salaries. It's better if you do the same. Thus your life here will go on smoothly. I won't say another word, otherwise you will take me for a mad woman.

-And if not?

-Then you'll blame yourself.

-One more question, - He refused to believe her and at the same time wanted to get to the heart of the matter. – Why have you left this splendid house and rented an apartment in the suburbs? I would say it is a great pity.

Alina's husband who stood nearby grumbled in a husky voice:

-Try it out and then we'll talk.

Alina stared at him reproachfully but didn't say a word.

-Oh, yes, one more thing. In our library you will find a good collection of literature about Malta. I would recommend you to read about the Order of Saint John, its tongues and the members. After all, the whole island was their territory and probably still is. There is a chance that you will discover something curious.

After they departed, Nikolay went to the office and started looking through the folders trying to define his responsibilities.

As he has settled in the house, he understood that his duties were not many. The main work was supposed to start at the beginning of summer, when they held an annual Russian summer school, for which students from different countries signed up year after year. In addition, he had to welcome a score of Russian teachers arriving from Moscow.

His apartment was at the very top of the mansion, connected with the rest of the building by a narrow, winding stairwell. He did not like that winding staircase, which looked so different from wide wooden carved stairwell connecting the first three floors of the house, but the apartment was spacious, well lit and comfortable, and he made up his mind to ignore the narrow stairwell.

In the old patrician mansion, silence reigned as if nobody had lived here for centuries, No one sat in the deep arm chairs, threw open the doors to the balconies decorating the light stone façade of the building.

Nikolay went down and entered the library where amidst the books stockpiled on the shelves, he found a brochure about the history of the house. The mansion existed since the second half of the 16th century.

-Very impressive, very, - he mumbled to himself.

His opinion about the house continued to grow: 'Centuries went by and the walls are as solid as they were at the start. Masons like these don't exist anymore'.

The Russian Cultural Center was founded in Malta in 1990 when the Maltese government came up with the idea of selling the dilapidated and unoccupied mansion on Merchants street.

During the reconstruction following the purchase of the house, the Russians transformed the inner courtyard into a concert hall. That gave them the possibility of organizing a summer school besides having occasional concerts.

Looking through the brochure and the photos illustrating the festive occasions and Russian classes, Nikolay understood that Alina and her husband worked hard and devoted much of their energy to the Center.

Here and there he came across the name 'Starki'. So, he was the first owner of the house, wasn't he? Still, some doubts clouded his brain. Then why did she procure the masses for his repose? And why did she go to the cathedral?

He has failed to answer the questions and decided to take a walk.

"Equally strange, she refused to stay in the mansion and moved out leaving Valleta altogether. I don't understand anything".

The weather was lovely. Seeing mimosa reminded him of Moscow where in spring at every street corner the florists were selling mimosa branches. He himself purchased innumerable bouquets for his girlfriends and colleagues. With the start of the season, mimosa arrives to Moscow in big volumes.

Here in Malta, he discovered how fluffy and tender fresh mimosa flowers could be, whereas during the transportation they turn into shriveled peas.

Nikolay was drawn to tall yellow bushes seen across the street behind a cast iron railing. After he had crossed the street, he realized the yellow forest has turned out to be a cemetery. It was adjacent to a noble looking edifice which housed the museum and had a common wall with the most famous building in Valletta – Saint John the Baptist Cathedral.

The old cemetery was not big, bearing the stamp of time and would look abandoned if not for the well preserved and well cared for graves, each of which had a medium-size stone cross with eight angles.

The whole complex occupied the full block between Republican and Merchants streets. Grass and wild flowers had sprung up on old graves, which, according to the dates, were all dug in 1565. Nikolay has heard about the Knights of the Order of Saint John and about the Great Siege.

Most likely those buried here in simple graves were the knights who perished in that ferocious war between Christians and the Ottoman Turks.

Once upon a time the graves had formed orderly rows, but now with the passage of centuries, the rows were twisted. As Nikolay strolled along one of the curves, it took him to the walls of a pretty building in Baroque style constructed of light color limestone, the same which was used in the construction of the Russian Cultural Center.

Still further, he discovered a side entrance to the cathedral, though after some hesitation, he decided not to go inside. The glorious weather persuaded him to stay outdoors and continue his walk.

The air was heavily saturated with the aroma of mimosa, the birds were singing and the sun was shining. The cemetery was narrow and long. It surprised him that in the very center of the city a potentially valuable piece of land was preserved for the cemetery and not used for modern construction. He noted admiringly: 'How they respect their dead'.

At the graves he looked at the names, hoping to find the former owner of the house, but obviously he was not there.

Once at home, he again took out the brochure and more attentively looked through the article about Sir Oliver Starki. He was the only Englishman in the Order, the Latin Secretary of the Grand Master Jean Pariso de la Valet and fought next to him throughout the Siege of 1565.

That night was tranquil and peaceful and Nikolay could not imagine how different his future nights in the house would be. Only once was his sleep interrupted by some loud mournful sighs sounding next to his pillow. Even after he jumped off the bed and turned on the light he heard the echo of restrained sobbing. If he were asked to characterize them, he would answer: that person is suffering, unable to express his grief loudly, instead he pours out his misery in stifled complaints. Believing himself dreaming, Nikolay put his head back on the pillow and fell asleep.

The next morning, Alina walked in to pick up the rest of her belongings.

Seeing his energetic and agile stride and activity, she smiled:

-Will you be here alone? Isn't your wife coming?

He dismissed her question, waving his hand:

-It has happened like that. I will be living here alone.

-Then you will need a dog. Believe me, this is not the place for a single person. It will be hard.

Nikolay scratched his head and smiled shyly:

-I suppose it is a good idea. But I don't know how to start looking for a companion dog. Firstly, we have to adapt to each other, I mean that our characters should match. I will think about your advice. Probably you are right, through up to now I've managed on my own.

Alina kept on looking at him:

- Will you accept my Rex? You can keep him up to July. We are returning for the summer school and for our dog it is better to stay put, I mean, in one place. He hates planes. Rex is a hairy beast, a Newfoundland. Very big and powerful. Next autumn he will leave with us for Moscow. But in summer he will help you to adapt to Malta.

Not even trying to hide his astonishment, he asked:

-Is it really so hard to adjust to the place?

-Still you have no idea how useful Rex will be.

As usual, Nikolay made an attempt to turn the serious conversation into a joke and dismissed her suggestions shrugging his shoulders when the solemn expression on Alina's face obliged him to fall still:

-If you like you can laugh at me. I assure you that I will be happy to see you laughing in July upon our return.

After she was gone, Nikolay gave a sign of relief: 'Finally alone. I will get some rest, peace and tranquility'.

He looked around: 'From now on, this is my home, at least for the next three years. And if I perform well, it might be longer'.

When he had concluded the inspection of the mansion, he went out to the courtyard, or what was left of it after the concert hall was completed. Two small outhouses were locked and he had no keys to them, thus postponing their inspection till the next day.

The walls of the Concert hall were adorned with the pictures of students and teachers, proving that the school kept the same contingent of professors year after year. It became obvious why Alina was certain she would be back in July.

The formal dining room was furnished with antique quality carved sideboards and display cases, where behind the glass he could see white gold trimmed porcelain. In the first reception the bookshelves were lined with works of the Russian classics, Pushkin and Tolstoy.

He loved everything except for that narrow winding stairwell needed to climb his apartment.

"What nonsense! How much time will I spend in my place? Besides, the whole house is mine. If I want, I can dine downstairs, work in the study and read in the library". – Nikolay was pleased with his logic.

Altogether the Russian Center engaged three Maltese whose different duties were not clearly indicated. In addition to them, as Alina pointed out to Nikolay, during the receptions organized by the Center, and that would be his duty, he was permitted to hire additional help. This was specified in the business expenses account. She even insisted that he could go over the board with the expenses, because the Maltese respected generosity.

After the work was finished, three Maltese were leaving. He was alone in that big and silent house.

The next day Alina came back with an enormous dark furry dog next to her.

One look at the calm and noble creature was enough to appreciate his character. The dog generated the impression of being kind and understanding.

Nikolay even suspected that Rex knew what was expected of him. The dog lazily waved his tail, sculptured like a palm tree branch, sniffed at his feet and, considering his mission fulfilled, settled on the carpet near the entrance.

-That was his favorite place, - Alina started and caught herself, - until...

-Until what? – Nikolay moved closer to her.

-Nothing, nothing. I suppose I have to go. My husband is waiting. She was speaking hurriedly, avoiding answering his question:

-Feel at home. Remember that you are the boss.

Nikolay replied:

-Frankly, I am very grateful to you. For Rex. I know how hard it is for an owner to part with his dog even for a short time. In my youth, I was a hunter and had a hunting dog, an English setter. He was my friend and my assistant. As for my part, I promise to take a good care of him. Let's hope we will become friends.

-And I can promise that he will take a good care of you. – With these words, Alina left.

Nikolay was looking at the dog and the longer he looked the more he liked him.

Rex was drowsing, or just pretending, because from time to time he opened eyes and met Nikolay's gaze as if reproaching him: 'Why are you staring at me? What is the big deal? You'd better invite me for a walk".

-You are right. Let's go. You will show me around, the streets, the area, your favorite places.

He rose and fixed a leash to the dog collar left by Alina.

-After the walk when we are back, I will treat you to tasty bones.

Rex understood, quickly jumped to his feet and sat next to the door, showing his complete readiness to leave.

They left the house and went in the direction of the Small harbor.

Nikolay was eager to find the dock where the Russian ships anchored during their short stops on the way to the Southern Seas. Rex ran eagerly and surely as if the road was familiar to him. They approached the houses perched along the hill and looking at the sea, descended along a narrow trail to the harbor and came upon the territory of the port. Storage buildings, piles of fishnets in disarray, wooden counters, everything proved that Valletta still preserved its activity as a fishing-port, not only as a commercial and naval port. At present the docks were empty.

Not far in front of a car parking he spotted the pleasure harbor for small boats and yachts. Nikolay stood quietly absorbing the beauty of the boats painted bright blue with an intense ochre line running along the rim of the deck. The vessels clearly competed with the intense blue of the sea waves, lazily licking the stone barriers under the warm afternoon sun. He turned back and admired the illuminated spires and the cupola of Saint John the Baptist Cathedral, crowning the cube shape of the Cathedral.

Rex swiftly moved between recently painted and drying ships, fixed high on the rafters. The beach was empty. Nikolay sat on a wooden decking, closed his eyes and let himself be carried away by rhythmic motion of the waves, mixed with husky screams of seagulls.

He drowsed, warmed up by the sun rays, Rex lay next to him, putting his big head on his lap as if inviting Nikolay to caress his hairy head.

Evening breeze started, the waves banged more vigorously and the first clouds came up presaging the swift sunset. Nikolay rose to his feet and noticed that the Cathedral did not look bright and light golden. The sun was gone and the edifice turned much darker. The crimson red paint of the central cupola became visible, and above it a small tower dominated, also dark red, crowned with a cross.

When they arrived home, Rex took his place at the entrance, while Nikolay went up to his apartment. It was time to unpack. He was taken aback that the curtains were open and the room was heated. But it must have been the mistake of a maid, he decided. She looked after the building and kept it in order.

The next day, he made the acquaintance of the cook. As Nikolay understood, all three Maltese employees did not live in Vallette. Every evening after work, they returned home to the suburbs.

Nikolay's attempts to find out why they preferred the suburbs were met by short responses: 'It is too expensive here', or 'We like it more'.

Looking at the dog, drowsing at his place Nikolay unexpectedly felt he missed Moscow. His friends, his daughter were all there and here he had nobody to say a word. He fancied how next summer she would come here and spend her vacation with him. How happy she would be to get acquainted with the island and how happy he would be to take her around.

Certainly, she will like it here, he thought.

In the library, while looking through the program for summer activities he realized it wouldn't be easy going. The key note of the season was Pushkin's anniversary. The poet's jubilee was celebrated in June in every Russian Cultural center in the world. Next would be the arts festival, for which he was promised to get a folk dance group and two theater troupes. He needed to prepare the flyers and send invitations to the city hall.

Several hundred Russian families had settled on Malta and the Centre was trying to get them involved in different types of activities. They had created a poetry competition for children. The winners were traditionally invited to Moscow.

Men need to be busy, otherwise they can get depressed easily. Doing future planning, Nikolay was cheered up.

The next morning, according to protocol, he went to the city hall to introduce himself to the mayor and to his assistant and to invite them to the Centre.

Rex walked next to him. Sometimes he turned his head and looked around as if asking whether there were other dogs nearby. Nikolay himself paid attention to the fact that they had not met a single dog. Though sometimes local cats crossed their way without arousing much interest from Rex.

When they came back, he was determined to finish up his unpacking and, saying good-buy to the Maltese he went up the stairs. His apartment was brightly lit by the sun and hot. Firstly bewildered, then with some apprehension, he cast a look at the windows. The curtains were pulled up and from the windows he was staring at the spires of the Cathedral towers and the cemetery, which was hidden by the blooming mimosa bushes. Before leaving in the morning he clearly recalled drawing the curtains and even recording that fact in his notebook. Could it be that someone else inhabited the house? Invisible and silent? But where?

The two small outhouses were locked, and inside the house, it was unrealistic for anyone to hide here day after day.

Examining the lock on his door, so primitive and shaky that anyone could open it with a simple Swiss knife it dawned on him to get a good solid lock. Close to the city gates, near the entrance to Valletta on the Republican square, there was a shopping mall with all kinds of stores. In one of them without wasting much time he bought a sturdy lock and door bolts.

The rest of the day was spent fixing a new lock. It required time because he door was massive, made of oak, surely quiet expensive, must have been brought here from outside. While busying himself with the lock, he grumbled at the door being so hard that it refused to yield to his instruments and efforts.

After two hours, the lock was fitted, adjusted to the key and Nikolay put his head on a pillow to have a rest.

When drowsing, he again heard some disturbing sounds and odd murmuring. But what astonished him most, they sounded as if the source of these worrisome pronouncements was located close to him, in the same room.

When he opened his eyes, he had a hard time fixing his gaze: the room was swaying, the ceiling was rising towards eternity as if there was open space above.

He called: 'Rex, where are you?' and when lifting his head instead of expected tender whining was met by silence. The dog was not in the room. He heard barking behind the locked doors.

« How could I forget about him and close the door?!" He opened the door and was met by happy Rex who jumped and attempted to lick his face.

They went down. Rex was eagerly running down the steps ahead. In the courtyard, Nikolay went directly to the outhouses. The night before he got the key from the cook and now tried to put it inside the key hole, as old as the key itself. With a big effort, he managed to turn it and the door opened. Inside it was dark, dusty and empty. Inadvertently it occurred to him that someone could conceal himself there and make tours of the house while everyone was away. In the other outhouse he detected heaps of papers, faded folders and broken flower pots. Trash.

Against the wall, broken chairs were stacked up; old Russian newspapers covered the floor. Rex was behind, whining, the fur on his neck and head rose. His tail was stretched as if he were in a set hunting for pheasants.

After the inspection was over he climbed to his apartment and checked again the solidity of the newly fixed lock.

This time, Nikolay and Rex chose a different direction for their walk. Feeling more secure and relaxed, he decided to behave like an ordinary tourist and visit the local sightseeing stars. Among the first were the local opera theater Manuel and the Anglican Saint Paul church.

Nikolay was a navy officer, who grew up in the Soviet Union, where every sign of religious devotion or interest was discouraged and even interrupted. So it happened that he remained quite indifferent to any religion and never went to church.

The day was drawing to a close and again the city in front of his eyes was turning from shimmering gold to bright ochre with unexpected splashes of orange shadows. The buildings acquired the dramatic sharp silhouettes as if they agreed to serve as the background for Caravaggio paintings.

Logically, it would be proper to get to the Cathedral and look at both Caravaggios if not at anything else. He was interested in art and was aware of the main treasure of Malta. The two masterpieces of the painter –that was all that the Maltese could preserve during these four centuries, which passed since Caravaggio lived and worked here. The rest of his output was gone, stolen or destroyed, like the master himself. He died on the Liguria coast near Genoa and his body was never found. 'The Beheading of Saint John the Baptist' and 'Saint Jerome' remained in the Cathedral and served as the main tourist attraction.

Strolling along the city which quickly was becoming deserted, Nikolay fell under the spell of a peculiar atmosphere, as if the streets were wrapped in some kind of mystery, as if they were trying to cover up something.

Malta looks like an attractive Mediterranean island with a pleasant climate, warm sea, Southern beauty and historic appeal, but at the same time it is filled with heaviness. He remarked that towards the end of the day the streets became quiet and still. The few children are gone and after the stores closed silence reigned, undisturbed by anything and anybody.

The Cathedral was open and Nikolay found both paintings by Caravaggio. 'The Beheading of Saint John the Baptist put him in a gloomy mood. Is there any connection between the city atmosphere and the subject of the canvas? The Cathedral adjoining the graveyard, the graves themselves and the vault where the canvas has hung for four hundred years looked as if they were part of the same event. The murder was transformed by the powerful hand of the painter into the reality of Valletta and reaches us centuries later.

A cruel murder created a strong impression. The longer he stared at it, the gloomier he was becoming. The painter depicted the Biblical story, as an ordinary incident, like a trivial scene with four participants. Judging by their face expressions and gestures, it was obvious that they were well aware of what a hideous act they were involved in. The crime had bound them together forever. The universe was plunged into darkness, turning into a sunless ruin, similar to the shady landscape of Valletta at night.

Nikolay almost crossed himself and hurried out of the Cathedral, just in time for the closing signal.

After a simple supper he went upstairs.

In the middle of the night, he was returned to reality by a loud noise coming from downstairs. He jumped up trying to figure out how someone could organize a feast in the house without his knowledge. Judging by the tinkling of china and clatter of glasses the guests enjoyed themselves enormously. A bit later he heard music. It was strange to his ears, something like church music, then singing followed, also plaintive which he could take for a local folklore. And still later he heard guitar strings. In spite of himself, he felt his heart was full of emotions. The feast lasted for a long time.

After some hesitation, Nikolay resolutely got up and pulled the door knob. It was stuck. Already in a panic, he strived hard, but all his efforts were fruitless. Time was passing painfully, reminding him of his previous struggles with that door. Finally at dawn, he succeeded in opening the door and discovered dead silence. Standing on the landing and looking down, he saw the dark well of the stairs without any hint of light. Neither could he distinguish any sound; no whisper, no music, no guitar.

At the entrance hall the dog crawled up, looking small and frightened. He was whimpering.

Nikolay took him by the collar and led him upstairs. The dog showed no resistance. On the contrary, he walked obediently as if demonstrating his guilt.

"Most likely, my neighbor invited her friends and they were feasting well after midnight. It is high time for us to become acquainted.—Coming to that conclusion, he went to bed.

But the next morning, he was busy and did not find an occasion to speak to the neighbor. The following days were quiet and he forgot about that strange incident and decided not to bother his neighbor.

Time was running smoothly, approaching the beginning of the Summer School. Rex looked tranquil and resumed his nightly walks around the house, after which he invariably returned to his favorite place at the entrance hall.

A Russian navy ship under the command of rear-admiral Shuvalov anchored in the harbor. According to custom, Nikolay invited the rear-admiral and his suite to a reception. Supper followed.

When the guests settled at the table, suddenly all of them clearly heard laughter, talk and clinking of dishes and glasses as if someone else in the same dining room was celebrating a birthday anniversary.

Everyone at the table fell silent, but unlike his guests, host had to pretend everything was normal, that he was not surprised and was well aware of the situation. What upset him most was Rex's whining. The dog was waiting behind the closed door begged to be let in.

-Oh, those are my neighbors, nothing to be surprised. It is not worth paying attention, - Nikolay's words did not seem to have any effect on the stunned guests.

They kept on turning their heads, trying to comprehend where the noise was coming from. He noted that doubts remained, that his explanations were not believed, and that the festive atmosphere was destroyed. He himself attentively listened to everything and was at a loss to grasp the source of the noise.

In the morning his neighbor, a thin elderly lady in a black skirt and a black kerchief on her white hair, stopped him with the question:

-You have such a good time here, with daily parties, music and guests. I suppose it is all done to celebrate your moving in, the house-warming, isn't that it?

However, seeing his puzzled expression she fell silent, and he could catch a glimpse of insidious satisfaction in her eyes.

-I was sure the parties were in your house.

The old woman kept on staring at him:

-Sir, I have been living alone for many-many years. In my 80s, I have no desire for noisy parties.

I won't say anything except for one fact. That was not me. Surely.

She looked askance at Rex, as if fearing the dog could understand her words and crossed the street beckoning Nikolay to follow her.

-The mansion of Oliver Starki is enchanted. We all know that it was chosen by ghosts for a very long time. Probably, these were rumors, but since my childhood I heard that they issued a warning for anyone wishing to restore it. The warning was: do not touch it. Thus nobody did for over 100 years. But you Russians don't believe in such nonsense, ghosts, spirits, apparitions, do you? I won't add another word, except that because of this ill fame nobody wanted to buy it. The Russians acquired it quite cheaply. Now you will be sharing the mansion with the ghosts.

When the house was a wreck, it was quiet, the ghosts were not heard or seen, and nobody organized late suppers.

As soon as I heard music, I suspected the apparitions have come back. Though for a while I had hopes that your and your friends are involved in those evening banquets. Now I realize that it is all the tricks of Oliver.

In our city everyone hopes to sell an apartment or a house. If you take prices, they are moderate, but nobody finds any customers. People are leaving Valletta. Look around and you will pay attention at the number of 'for sale' ads.

She lowered her voice still more:

-Officially the tenants of the apartments and houses don't complain. They whisper to each other. Probably you are not aware, but in Malta there exists a law, according to which you can be taken to court if you say that someone's property is inhabited by ghosts. Thus, you cast malicious fame on the property and destroy its value.

She entered her house and Nikolay remained dumfounded. He shook his head:

-It is amazing what kind of nonsense one can pick up from old bags.

The evening was beautiful, tranquil and serene. As it had become their custom, Nikolay and Rex went back to the harbor. He settled comfortably on the stone steps and watched the evening mist enwrapping the bay, approaching the seashore and bringing the evening freshness, then floating in semi transparent rivulets in between the narrow streets, climbing the hillocks.

Going back home, he for the first time looked around and discovered that his neighbor was correct. The houses along the streets had a number of offers, white and yellow posters about sale or rent. Judging by the uninhabitable look of the properties, it was obvious that the owners put their house for sale some time ago. Boarded up windows, scratched front doors, rusty balcony grilles gave the streets a look of desolation and the trees, unattended and overgrown, sticking out from behind stone fences, increased the sad picture.

Nikolay was attentive and now, after the information and hints, he sensed something peculiar about the city. In addition to the absence of night life so natural for any capital of the world, when the citizens finish their day's work and want to pour their energy in the entertainment, he began perceiving other strange signs. After the tourists disappeared and the souvenir shops closed their shutters, the town turned into a ghost shelter. It looked as desolate as a stagnant swamp.

The vision of evening dreariness was magnified by the public parks, where the number of monuments to the fallen rivaled the few trees. These memorials commemorated the participants of the endless battles fought here during centuries. Even the streets were named after the dead, with the rare exceptions like his own- Merchants street and the main one- Republican street.

He was standing near the house, staring at the cemetery across the street: 'What a drastic change in my mood, -he said to himself. – The first days here I liked everything and now even the handsome mimosa bushes scare me, as if they exhale chilly and poisonous waves.

For an obvious reason mimosa thrives here. Like specters. We, the living mean nothing to them. We are obstacles on their way and they kick us like stones along the road. What if they are here on the cemetery, across the street? Quite an arrangement. They lived here, were buried here and we exist under their watchful gaze'.

He hardly restrained him making a sign of the cross. 'What a story. One more day and I will turn to God for help'.

That evening he stayed up later than usual, preparing the plan for the next day. To his surprise, the dog followed him upstairs refusing to sleep on his carpet at the entrance.

-Rex, why don't you stay there? It is cooler.

Without looking at him, the dog kept on climbing the steps, walked into the bedroom and lay down between the bed and the window. Only then did he look at Nikolay and waved his tail as if saying:

-I won't take much room.

Still under the influence of the conversation with his neighbor, Nikolay locked the door, again admiring the solidity of the new lock. 'No, no, -he was saying to himself. - Ghosts don't exist. They are all the inventions of lonely old women. My head is slightly turning and vision is foggy, but I am sure this is the result of the unfamiliar place and loneliness.

He tried to fall asleep. It felt as if the dog was doing the same. He was turning and turning, his whining sounded plaintive and he was breathing heavily. Nikolay wanted to caress him, but the dog crawled under the bed.

-What are you doing here? - He was telling Rex when suddenly heard such a howling that his hair stood up. That was not Rex, because at that moment Rex snarled and tried to bite his hand. Someone was standing behind the door. Nikolay felt his blood was turning to ice.

Another howling sent shivers along his spine. He was sure someone was in the bedroom.

In a fraction of a second, Rex scrambled from under the bed, jumped and descended on Nikolay. Now it was his turn to jump and utter a moan. Only the familiar thick fur persuaded him it was Rex.

The dog was lying, tightly pressed against Nikolay's body. They both were shuddering.

Any thought about falling asleep was forgotten and Nikolay was waiting for another awful howling. Beyond any doubt, it was doomed to come.

Someone made an attempt to open the door as he could judge by scratches of claws.

His mind was working with a feverish speed: 'My service dagger! Where is it? Is it still inside my suitcase?

Is it in the other room? Or is it here? I can't get to that room. What shall I do? Something! Fast! But what? '

By rank he was a captain and was entitled to have a full parade dress together with a service dagger. He never could imagine that the dirk would be needed in such circumstances.

Time was going by. Rex had stopped shaking. But they both strained their ears, expecting to hear the dreadful howling. Very carefully, slowly and noiselessly Nikolay stretched out his hand and turned on the light. Looking around, he tried to guess where this sound was coming from. At the same time he was evaluating his chances.

Except for the razor and scissors, he had no other weapon of self defense. Yes, Rex's fangs. But judging by the dog's panic, it looked as if he had to defend them both.

Behind the door the sound of retreating steps encouraged him to breathe and to relax.

Dawn was breaking and the birds began to chatter and sing. Nikolay heard the screeching wake up call coming from a rooster settled near by. His vigilant summons were transformed into a piercing loud scream, victorious and cheerful.

Still Nikolay did not dare to stir. Similarly the dog was motionless, though judging by his moving ears, he stayed on the alert.

The birds rejoiced and sang loudly before departure for villages and fields. Nikolay put down his feet: 'I have a lot to do. The officers from the cruiser are coming. Before their visit I have to go and check what they need'.

He stole up to the door and saw Rex jumping off the bed. His mind registered the amazing lightness with which this enormous furry body managed to land so quietly. The dog's tail was placed between his legs, his ears stretched forward and his eyes were glittering.

Behind the door silence reigned. Nikolay put his ear to the keyhole and heard nothing. Very carefully, he turned the key in the lock, but as before it refused to turn. He pressed the key harder. The result was similar. Then he strained his hand, bent his back muscles and pushed the key with all his strength.

Rex followed his movements very attentively.

-Damn it! How jammed it is! - Nikolay murmured.

Late in the morning under the bright sun rays he managed to open the door and got out. Rex stood behind lifting his nose and sniffing. His fur again rose and eyes were burning. He dared to dash forward, but immediately stepped back.

How Nikolay would love to get back to Moscow right now, without delay. Take the first plane out, as fast as possible from this damn place, without waiting another day. To hell with this poisonous yellow mimosa! He would welcome the snow storms and cold and ice. Only they are capable of sweeping clear this evil force.

On the back of the door, he noticed dark spots which could be left either by claws or by ink. Rex approached the traces, sniffed and growled. When Nikolay brought water and began cleaning, the dark spots spread along the surface of the door.

Determined not to mention this incident to anyone, he was on his way out when downstairs, he discovered a letter from Alina Zorina.

"Now you know the secret of the house and understand me. I hope you have begun going to the Cathedral and ordered the services for the repose of Sir Oliver's soul. Otherwise, you will suffer. The house is inhabited by ghosts. The main one is the former owner sir Oliver. Like you we also refused to believe it for a very long period, over two years. Don't repeat our mistake. Finally, we could not tolerate it anymore and hastily ran to Vittoriosa.

My husband decided to behave rationally and the first thing he did was to look in the local archives for the will of Sir Oliver. When we read it, we understood his anger. All his enormous estate was left to the Cathedral with only one condition –to serve masses for his soul and for the souls of his friends. That should last till the end of the universe.

I must admit that I was impressed by the honesty of the Maltese. They followed literally his will up to the end of the last war. But after 1946 they stopped. Imagine the awful destruction here caused by the Allied bombings. The death, rubble. Who would care about the wishes of a person who lived 400 years before?! Sir Oliver started reminding us about himself. First humbly, then more aggressively. At that moment we moved into his house. After my husband saw the will, we paid for the masses. However, he did not stop frightening us, but demanded more and more. We gave up and left the house and the city.

He did not bother us in Vittoriosa.

If you don't want to pay for the masses, you'd better leave the house. After all, it is his house and he has the right to insist on keeping promises.

Our dog is horrified by the ghosts. Be kind to him and don't leave him outside the apartment. Otherwise, at the first opportunity he will run way. It has happened already.

I wish you luck and peace".

Nikolay put the letter down and became pensive. So, that is true. As he had suspected in his heart of hearts, at the same time refusing to accept it. They do exist. In his brain of a Soviet military officer such a thing could find no lace. The other world? The nether world? But he witnessed it and heard it. Still, he could not accept it. This evening he had to receive guests and explain to them the music and singing and drinking party of the invisible participants in the same room.

If he were ready to accept this strange reality, then he had better go to the Cathedral and do as Alina advised.

He decided to write her a letter and ask for help. Should he leave the house, though he was reluctant to do it, to say nothing about the sense of defeat and humiliation? No, not that. An officer has no right to give up, otherwise he will lose his honor. An officer won't be scared and chasted out by evil spirits. He will stay in the house till the end. No matter what happens, at any cost. In spite of all the threats.

Payment for the masses of someone who lived 400 years ago is the condition of calm life here, however crazy that sounded. But if that is the price, he should accept it. Then he will live here. If not?

«I can't tell a soul about what is happening in the house. Only to you. People will take me for a mad man. You are a woman and it is easier to accept the cock-and-bull from you. But I am a military man. I feel very stupid asking you for help. Is it really the only solution to leave the house? Nothing else? "

The closing phrase sounded like a scream in the desert.

Even when he was hunting, alone in the forest, he had not been that scared. The world in the forest was real and followed rules. If one knows them and respects them, then his life is not in danger and he enjoys close contact with nature. But here what kind of nature did he bump into?

After folding the letter he admitted to himself that he was scared by something which was beyond his perception. Could it be that all these apparitions were tricks of Oliver Starki? He knew that having Rex was life saving. He would not have lasted a day here without a dog. Even a frightened dog as Rex was.

He jumped:

-I am an officer and not going to be scared by somebody's ghost.

Again he went to the cemetery looking for Starki's grave and again could not find it. Who knows whether it was ever there, - he wondered.

-Probably in the museum, they will give me an answer, - he guessed. – Or at least I can look at the portrait of the man. They must have it.

Soon he was staring at the darkened portrait of the 50-year old austere man in dark formal attire with a white grooved collar and piercing eyes. His gaze seemed to follow him in the room, no matter where he stood and moved.

Finally he got so uncomfortable that making a playful gesture, he murmured:

-Dear Sir, I am grateful for your hospitality, – and left.

At the Cathedral he scribbled Starki's name on a piece of paper and put $10 in a special slot.

When he asked Alina how much he should leave to the Cathedral, she replied:

-At your discretion.

For some time the remedy worked, because the weird elements did not give him reason for anxiety. Rex looked relaxed, did not sniff every corner in the house and did not crawl under the tables and chairs. Nikolay was persuaded that at last a calm existence has begun.

And then, unexpectedly, he got an invitation to visit an acquaintance in a village not far from Valletta. He decided to take Rex. The dog looked happy jumping along until they came across a cart pulled by three mules. As Nikolay came up to the coachman he welcomed him, but to his surprise did not hear any reply.

Suddenly Rex stopped and began barking, trying to attack the cart. His eyes were burning and his fur rose.

Here we go again, - Nikolay thought drearily. He closed his eyes, hoping that the cursed vision would disappear. And that was true. When he opened the eyes, the damn cart was not there anymore. Rex stood calmly, the road was empty and dark.

-Let's hurry up. Otherwise we'll be late, - he addressed the dog, who in response contentedly waved his tail.

They entered the village and found the street. At the end of it the same cart was moving slowly, its wheels producing a squeaky sound. Nikolay and Rex watched motionlessly how the silent coachman on a pile of hay was passing the house they were going to enter.

The dog was shivering and whining, however, he did not attempt to run to it or to attack the sinister cart. How could Nikolay blame the dog while he himself did not dare to take a step forward? What should he do? Was there any chance for his friend to notice something strange and come out or would he stay here and wait till the cart disappeared. Then how would he explain to his friend the delay was caused by a bizarre incident?

And even if he turned and ran home where were the guarantees that the same cart would not be waiting for them in Valletta?

He passed his hand along the dog's back:

-In that house people are waiting for me and for you and they have prepared delicious bones. Tonight I have no desire to return to Valletta. We'll do it tomorrow when it will be sunny and bright.

Saying that he made a sign of the cross, then another one deliberately and meaningfully and bent his head:

-Please go back to the netherworld where you have emerged from. I give you a promise that tomorrow in the

Cathedral I'll order the mass for the repose of your soul. But now let us pass and enter the house and let us spend this night in peace.

The ominous cart and three mules vanished as if dissolved in the night.

After several calm and uneventful weeks, one night Nikolay had a hard time falling asleep and decided instead of taking a sleeping pill to descend to the library and read. As soon as he made an attempt to go down the stairs, he stopped dumbfounded. Above the landing the chair was standing in the air. But how could it stand there? At the same time there was no other place for a chair on that small and narrow landing. It was obvious and probably logical that the chair did not stand, but was suspended in the air above the landing. In the obscure light its shape was clearly visible.

Nikolay descended one flight and wanted to grab the chair, but as soon as he touched it, he got such a powerful push that fell head over heels. When he opened the eyes, the first thing he noticed was the same chair, only now suspended above his head. He rose to his feet, groaning and passed his hands along his body trying to verify whether there were any broken bones. No, his body still was in one piece.

Now Nikolay became furious. Forgotten were his fears and horror and the esteem Sir Oliver excited in him.

He got so angry that could not even talk, but whispered in a low voice which sounded like the hissing of a snake.

-Not only do you disturb my nights and scare my dog, but now you push me down the stairs. I don't like it.

-Stop intervening in my life and let me entertain my guests. This house belongs to me, - he heard the dull expressionless voice.

-What?! You are dead!

-Fool! Don't you still realize that the world is shared by everybody, dead and alive. We occupy the same space.

-What do you need now? Shall I go to the Cathedral and order the masses?

-That is not enough. My friends also require attention. My money is enough for them all.

-Well, if you insist, I will do that. Just to be fair to you and to your friends.

-I will see.

The next time Nikolay returned to the Cathedral with a long list of names which he found in old books, all of them describing the epoch of Sir Oliver and the Great Siege.

When he paid for the masses, a group of Russian tourists was standing next to him listening to their guide who was described the treasures of the Cathedral while pointing to them Sir Oliver' vault.

Instead of listening to the guide, they turned their heads and stared at Nikolay. He smiled and hurried out, thus escaping any questions and curiosity.

In the museum he went straight to the hall where Sir Oliver's portrait was hanging. He had no special plan or intention. Without any thought he was scrutinizing the portrait which was very close, so close that he could see the eyelashes on the face. He lingered as if expecting something to happen. Time went by and he decided to make the first move:

-Here you see the receipts for the masses. – He took out the bluish blanks, - As I have promised, I will continue to order them, regularly, including for your friends. After some reflection, I agree with you. You are right. Money was donated and it is enough for masses. However, an injustice was committed and I intend to restore order. I promise that there will be no more interruptions in the services, but in return I ask you to give me peace.

Sir Oliver waved his hand stretching out of a long black sleeve with grooved cuff and was waving to him.

He stopped murmuring and dashed to the door, but at the last moment at the threshold stopped open-mouthed. The portrait was smiling, more precisely grinning, showing dark rotten teeth.

Holding the jamb of the tall polished door, Nikolay sank to the floor.

The last thing he remembered was the warm dog fur. He caressed Rex and complained about the cruel knight Sir Oliver, Rex replied in a soft comforting voice which relieved his fear and agitation. Under the stream of pleasing sounds he was drowsing before falling asleep. The room was lit by dazzling blue light and his bed slowly rose to the air and swung.

Saint Feuillien from Le Roeulx

In the Belgian village of Le Roeulx, every three years a big feast is organized to commemorate St Feuillien.

The Irish monk Feiullien arrived in a land populated by the *Belgas* in the seventh century to proselytize and introduce the pagans to the Christian faith. The festivities in his honor were first recorded in the eleventh century, when the Pope raised Feuillien to the rank of saint. The event played an important part in the life of the province. The morning procession along the streets of Le Roeulx and the evening show, performed by scouts from the local schools served as the main draw for locals and tourists.

Le Roeulx bordered on a sacred forest, where hermits and monks settled in the early Middle Ages. They built chapels and monasteries, which were ravaged during the time of the French revolution.

On the other side of the village, there was an impressive old castle surrounded by an enormous park. Once upon a time, it belonged to the noble family of the counts de Croy who left their motherland during the French revolution and never came back. For many years, it stood empty.

Every three years the property and the park sprang to life. On a vast green lawn, the summer theatre was erected. Chairs were placed in rows in front of a wooden stage, behind them, tables laden with food and drink.

According to established tradition, the day started in the local cathedral, which was named after St Feuillien. Following a short service, a wooden sculpture of the Saint was carried by four parishioners along the streets of Le Roeulx, with Father Stephan at the head of the procession.

The procession was coming to an end when suddenly a rustling sound was heard, as if a flock of doves descended from the bell tower. Those who carried the wooden sculpture looked up and saw a vision of the flying figure of a monk. Confused, they dropped the effigy and it fell on Father Stephan, who had also raised his head when he heard the commotion.

Father Stephan had to be taken to his bed and the doctor was summoned. But the sculpture was not damaged, and the rumors which started after the incident quickly stopped.

Fifteen children were well prepared for the evening performance and the three teachers who accompanied them were pleased. As a final touch, a short wooden staircase was constructed which led from the theater to the stage. The evening promised to be warm and agreeable, and everyone looked forward to the entertainment.

The spectators assembled in the hall. Gradually everyone stopped talking and gazed ahead.

After the curtain rose, the audience saw on the stage a young boy aged about 12 in a brown cassock with white belt and a hood pulled over his eyes. He was listening to four other monks played by boys of the same age.

"Why are you leaving us? We will feel lonely and lost without you, Brother."

The boy, whose name was Leon performed the role of St Feuillien. His parents were sitting in the front row, their pride apparent on their faces.

"My vocation is calling me," Leon replied. "I have to leave you, because here my obligations are fulfilled, but there across the sea the pagans need me. They need a pastor."

The boys sang *a capella* the psalm, "God, protect him." Leon joined them and after a tearful parting left the stage.

The play continued. Leon stood in the middle of the stage and three boys held a piece of blue cloth aloft, creating the waves of the North Sea. Thus, Feuillien crossed the sea and found himself on the continent. After long wandering, he arrived in the province of Haineau. A fellow traveler gave him some advice, "Brother, you should go to the Belgas. They are all pagans and will keep you busy."

The young actors stood on the stage dressed in medieval outfits. The girls wore long skirts, white laced caps, shoes with wooden soles. The boys wore dark long tunics with waist girdles and flat hats, sleeveless vests and boots.

Walking back and forth along the stage, they waited for Brother Feuillien to talk. Leon wore the same brown cassock. At times he lowered the hood, because he was hot and excited.

The parents of the actors in the audience enjoyed looking at their sons and daughters. They exchanged remarks and smiled, amused to hear children delivering parts of the sermons and pretending to be adults.

The scenes followed one after the other. In most of them, Feuillien was preaching, introducing the Gospel to the pagans and gradually winning over their hearts.

On the stage, the scenery took the form of a silhouette of a village house and two tall, leafy trees.

In between the scenes, the audience could hear hymns and psalms of meditation, lamentation and praise to God. The three teachers stayed behind the stage and never came out. The whole show was acted at by the children.

In the next scene, Brother Feuillien was seated, surrounded by his pupils. "Listen to me and through me you will approach our Lord. There is nothing more sacred than love. If your soul possesses no love, it is dying, one particle after another. When it dies, life loses sense. There is no bigger love than love for those close to you and devotion to our Lord."

It felt as if a soft breeze was passing along the hall. The eyes of some were filled with tears. Children moved closer to their parents, and wives to their husbands.

The teachers admired how well Leon played his role. He was around twelve, but he entered the spirit and the personality of St Feuillien so persuasively that he looked older.

Leon continued, "Another most important feature is bravery. Everybody needs to have it: monks, priests, parishioners. Your route is difficult, but many people passed this way before you, and many will follow after you. If you are courageous, you will bear anything."

The curtain went down and the audience sat in silence, absorbing what they had just heard. At that moment, Father Stephan entered the theater and, moving quietly, took a place in the last row.

He had spent this day in bed. He did not feel well and from time to time strange visions appeared before him. It could be his imagination. Obscure spots blended into a human figure clad in a cassock.

He took out some old books and studied them. The texts persuaded him that the incident with the wooden figure was not accidental and he had better research it, seeking its special meaning. His memory told him that this never happened to him before, though he participated in the processions for years and years. In these books he found the exact date of St Feuillien's death. It confirmed what he had suspected, that the festivities were organized on the anniversary of his death. Still, he reflected, it looked strange. He must go to the evening show. Groaning and supporting his body with a cane, Father Stephan left his house. He did not want to admit it to himself, but he had a premonition that something might happen.

After the curtain rose again, the audience saw two painted silhouettes of the houses and two trees bending above them. It was early morning and Brother Feuillien walked along the sacred forest towards the village of Le Roeulx, where he had agreed to meet his followers.

Suddenly, from behind the scene, a group of actors

rushed out. They were dressed in shabby rags, their faces painted black and they wore oversized furry hats. Their eyes were shinning ominously.

The hall went silent. Even the children, sitting next to their parents, stopped talking. The menacing appearance of the gang of robbers was heightened by the long knives which they were brandishing in front of Leon, shouting, "Quick, quick! Everything you possess, give it to us right now. We know that you've collected money from the peasants. Now it is ours. Fast, give us everything!"

Four boys surrounded Leon, who tried to get free, but in vain. They held him tightly.

"We have no time to bother with you. Fast, otherwise, you'll regret you ever were born."

In no time, they turned his pockets inside out and finding them empty, began demanding that he take off his cassock. Leon attempted to resist.

"I beg you not to hurt me. Great misfortune will befall you."

Instead of an answer, he heard the thieves' laughter.

"For you, it will be the start of eternal torture. While I will enter Paradise, God's kingdom, you'll end up in Hell. Please give me a little time to turn you to God! To our Jesus Christ! When you repent your crime, it will be too late."

The thieves did not listen to him. One was searching his body. "We shall see now," he said with a grimace, pulling off the monk's cassock.

The other one at that moment hit the monk, causing him to fall.

The hall burst into an emotional display. The spectators were distraught. Children sobbed. Darkness descended on the stage.

Just then from behind the chestnut trees a bright orange moon came out and lit up the sky. Its light deepened the shadows in the park. The audience turned around, fearing something unknown was approaching. But the tables laden with food and drink were still there. Behind them, the waiters stood ready to serve them as soon as the feast began. Gradually the spectators calmed down.

For the final scene of the show, the actors prepared a big effigy of the monk, dressed in the same brown cassock, and with this they replaced Leon at the moment when he was expected to fall to the ground.

Everything went as planned. Under the cover of darkness and the orange moon, Leon crawled along the side of the stage and descended by the small wooden staircase, hiding himself just below the stage.

According to the script, the robbers now understood that the monk was penniless and in fury killed him. The show was supposed to end with the apotheosis of Saint Feuillien. He would sit on the stage dressed in white among his followers.

When the actors playing the roles of the bandits bent down to check on Feiullien, they screamed, "He is alive, alive!" and rushed from the stage.

Knowing that these words were not in the script, the teachers ran onto the stage and approached the big doll lying in a heap on the floor. The audience held its breath. "Alive!" screamed startled teachers and set out running.

The parents sitting in the first row hurried to the stage by the narrow staircase, knocking into each other; they stared at the lying doll. Others pulled away their crying children.

The spectators pushed away their seats and started running. The hall was filled with commotion, when unexpectedly; the figure of a huge monk blocked their passage.

He soared into the air, not very high, but his movements were swift. His cassock rose behind him, forming a kind of a cloud. The spectators came to a halt.

A voice thundered: "I call for you. Come, closer, closer, draw near and look." From behind the bushes, four figures dressed as actors in the evening performance glided by. They hovered in midair.

'I was long waiting for your repentance. Do you see the results of what you have committed? Repent! Repent!" The voice reverberated.

'I was waiting for your repentance for centuries."

Sobbing, groaning, wailing broke out in the audience. People were frozen in fear. The yelling became louder. It seemed that the shadows tried to get loose and float away, but an invisible force prevented them. The monk then said: "Do you remember that I predicted your eternal torments. You did not believe and mocked me. Do you believe me now?"

'Yes, we believe you, saintly father, we believe! Pardon us!'

The phantoms were still floating above the stage.

'Centuries-long tortures have persuaded me to absolve you. I accept your repentance."

The figure slowly drifted over the summer theater. His cassock whirled behind him like dense smoke.

The four apparitions turned into dust and fell to the ground. Within minutes, the rain started and washed away every trace of them.

Two Pine Trees, A Love Story

The fire was getting closer and closer. It was a fierce fire that devastated everything around -trees, bushes, undergrowth. It was approaching two pine trees perched on the edge of the forest in a small valley.

One was a mature, magnificent tree, tall, straight, with gradually descending branches which created a regular triangle similar to what children draw in kindergartens. Hardy, resilient, with healthy, shiny cones hidden sheltered between strong sharp needles. Next to it and leaning against the strong, powerful trunk was a slender young tree with graceful branches waving freely because they were fragile, and with bright green needles. It looked as if both trees were growing from the same spot, as if their roots were intertwined under the ground just like their lower branches in the air.

The fire was getting closer, the strong hot wind was blowing persistently bringing the fire closer to two pine trees.

In the path of the fire, trees were burning, with loud cracking sounds and explosions.

The vestiges of the forest were smoldering, discharging black and white smoke.

'Mother,' whispered the young, slender tree. 'Help me. I am so hot that I can't breathe. It is frightening'.

The big, strong tree spread its immense wind-like branches and wrapped the daughter.

The young tree felt cool, took a deep breath and murmured: 'Thank you.'

But the ferocious fire did not stop. It was getting closer and closer. The dry grass at the base of the big pine tree was touched by a smoldering brand and in no time the lower branches were ablaze.

The daughter was crying: 'I am in pain. It hurts me, it is torture. Help me!'

The big tree made a desperate effort, bent over and its body encircled the trunk of the small tree. Thus, it was protected from the fury of the fire.

Little by little the fire stopped at the very edge of the forest, on the hill, somehow refusing to descend the hill. The night came, a stinking smoky night. Rain brought relief to the devastated forest or what remained of it.

The mother whispered: 'Are you well, my daughter? The danger is gone. No more heat and smoke'.

'When winter comes I will be cold. I have no more needles. I am afraid I will freeze to death'. She started crying.

The big pine tree whispered: 'Don't cry, my daughter. I will give you my warmth and you'll never be cold. My branches have protected you from the fire and my needles will protect you from the cold.

Thus, two pine trees stood at the same hilly side on the edge of the forest amidst a sad, tragic landscape of burnt trees: the fearful young one, fragile and weak, and big one, burnt, scorched, ginger as a fox, resembling in the color of its branches a dead autumn swamp. And from its burnt branches bright green needles on elongated slim branches were emerging.

People came and said in amazement: 'We need to free this young pine tree from that dead heavy trunk... It will produce cones, seeds, populate the area and will resurrect the forest'.

They tried to free the daughter from the mother's embrace but could not without damaging the young tree. Two pine trees were turned into one and there was no way to separate them.

People agreed they had witnessed a miracle and left the two trees in peace.

Avocado

Nick was looking out of the window watching the heavy rain splash on the cobblestones below. His colleague's remark seemed apt: 'Brussels rains are famous for their duration and you'd better be prepared."

Remembering this warning, he decided to check the weather forecast. But instead of looking at the weather in Belgium, where he found himself at this particular moment, he looked at the weather forecast in Turin which he had to leave not long ago.

Studying the pictures of the yellow sun, scattered white clouds framing the picture, he sighed. As he had expected, the weather in Turin was sunny with a temperature of 24 degrees C.

He lowered his head, not wishing to look outside. The reverberating glass panels told him what was waiting out there. If by some magic he could find himself in Italy and absorb for a short moment the warmth of the caressing sunrays, then he would believe the sun was still there. But magic did not exist.

Nick got up from his chair. It was time for him to leave this comfortable place and go to work. He would take his big, solid umbrella. The nearest subway stop was close and he needed a few minutes to get to it.

On the landing next to his door, he noticed a pyramid of tiles intended for the stairwell. The landlord was in a hurry to rent the apartments and had signed up tenants before he finished the renovation of the building. On Nick's floor, work continued, causing noise and dust. But the tenants, including Nick, tolerated the inconvenience because rent was modest and apartments were clean and refurbished.

His apartment was situated on the second floor, above a brasserie. On some evenings he spent a couple of hours in this eatery, where he would empty a few glasses of beer with his meal. Sometimes he even managed to play billiards in the back room. These were his contacts with the local society.

A few months ago when he moved to Brussels, he had big plans. He expected big changes in his life, felt he was at the threshold of something new and unknown. This new life did not scare him, but he did not anticipate the weather having such a big impact on his mood and energy.

Nick was at a loss to explain that influence. He was born in Yorkshire, a county not known for its pleasant climate. The locals could expect anything from nature and they got it, like prolonged rains, inundations, freezing and snowy winters. But for Nick, all this it was a matter of the past. Ever since he was ten years old, he had lived in other countries and rarely visited England. These countries were southern and warm.

First, with his parents he had lived in African countries. Then, on his own, he had spent a few years in South-East Asia. Later, after acquiring independence and getting married, he moved to Italy. He spent close to thirty years in

Turin. By that time, he had changed from a tall and lanky youth to a wide-shouldered, middle aged man with a bushy head of grey hair. His plump face used to be white, but after prolonged stays in sunny places had become permanently brown. Only the forehead hidden by hair betrayed its original color. Blue eyes, dark eyebrows which met at the bridge of his nose and a grey and black scraggly beard covering his chin completed the picture.

A job had brought him to Belgium. With his long experience in teaching, he had no problem getting a job in a place where he wanted to be.

Nick decided to make a break from exotic places and spend a few years in Western Europe.

In the first three months, everything worked well, even with the apartment. He quickly found what he was looking for: a refurbished place in the center, close to a Metro stop, stores, a farmers' market and entertainment.

The windows of his living cum dining room faced a lively square where people scurried about day and night, where restaurants and bars were open late and where every Sunday a huge market featuring local produce was set up. He felt himself part of this life, He had a feeling that he belonged to that active and noisy crowd and this inspired optimism in his soul.

The noise coming from the café on evenings did not disturb him and with these endless rains, there was little chance for the brasserie owners to set up an outside terrace for their clientele.

On the contrary, he liked the convenience and frequently ate his suppers there.

After a short hesitation, he went down along the narrow, freshly painted stairwell. Passing through the landing of the ground floor, where a back door from the café was open, he noticed a plant, stuck at the corner, next to a garbage bin. A slim and gracious avocado with two branches originating at the base was growing from a small ceramic pot. Its wide leaves hung sadly down, as if they did not have enough energy to stand up. Its upper shoots with barely visible bulges of future leaves were also hanging down. The whole picture created a feeling of desolation.

Nick slowed down and looked at the plant, which resembled a neglected child whom nobody needed and whose state was causing a feeling of embarrassment.

"What shall I do with you? Tomorrow you will be shipped to a garbage dump. An orphan can run away and you can't."

He smoothed his grey hair and contemplated the situation. It was strange that one of the tenants had disposed of a plant which obviously was in his possession for a few years. Who could it be? Besides himself, there were two tenants, both young and, as it seemed to Nick, not very inclined to cultivating plants.

Though he was in a hurry, something held him back. It was as if a silent call came from the sad plant, as if the drooping leaves unexpectedly vibrated and timidly asked for help.

He bent down and touched the soil in the pot. It was dry. Glancing at his watch and hesitating for a moment, he hurried to the exit, but at the last moment suddenly turned back. In his apartment, he filled in a water can and poured the whole container into the pot. Passing the plant again on his way out, he was startled by the changes in its appearance over just the past few minutes.

The plant revived. Its leaves shone and the faded branches raised themselves. It did not seem to be dying or destined to be dumped like a Christmas tree after the holidays.

Closing the door behind him and opening his umbrella while making an attempt to run, he told himself in a whisper: 'Now I have to run and even then I'll be late.' His heavy figure rushed down the escalator to a Metro train.

During the day his thoughts returned to that avocado sitting by itself, away from its African compatriots. Nick owned a few plants, but they were all back in Turin. Avocados were not among them. When he lived in Africa, he saw avocado plantations and it would feel strange to have one of these plants at home

In the evening, contrary to his habit, he did not stop at the café for a beer, but proceeded directly inside his building, eager to see whether the plant was still there. It was. Nobody had carried it away, attracted by its fresh look, deep green and shiny leaves and by the hint of its tropical origin showing in the multicolored trunk.

Nicholas knew that next morning, it was doomed for a dump fill in the Northern outskirts of Brussels. But the plant was still absorbing water provided by his generous impulse and suspected nothing of its future. The branches rose so high that they even formed a kind of a canopy, locking together.

The leaves softly rustled and seemed to turn towards him. Their whisper echoed in his heart resounding like a whole grove. He slowly climbed one flight of stairs. With each step he went slower and slower, then abruptly turned back and, carrying his big body two steps at a time, found himself next to the plant. He picked up the pot and, without looking around to see whether anyone saw him, hurriedly carried the plant into his apartment.

Judging by its strong trunk, the plant was a few years old. Even if it had lost a few leaves, the foliage looked thick and generous. Two spreading branches made it wide, and that must have been a reason why it was discarded.

'Will I have a place for the plant?' Nick thought. His apartment was not big and, at the moment, was spottily furnished. The best place for the plant would be on a wide windowsill in his living room. The large window would provide plenty of light and occasional sunny warmth.

"You will be the first tenant of the window sill," Nick said, putting the plant on it.

In three weeks, the avocado transformed itself into a thriving, happy plant. Nick believed that when he opened the door to the apartment it welcomed him with joyful rustling of its leaves. Every evening he washed the dust off the leaves, at the same time telling the avocado what had happened in the office. He now gave it a name – Caesar – by which he addressed it before recounting the day's events.

After a few pleasant, sunny days, the rain came back and darkness filled his apartment. Even the bedroom with its southern exposure was dimmed.

Nick decided that the plant needed if not sun, then at least fresh air and the company of nature.

In front of his building and behind the square there was a city park, where he occasionally spent time relaxing under the plantain trees.

Sunday came and he took the plant for a walk. In the park he sat at his favorite bench, putting the avocado next to it.

"Do you like it here?" he asked the plant. The leaves rustled in response and this brought happiness to his lonely soul.

It was not yet ten in the morning and the park was empty. Neither the children's playground nor the court for basketball was yet occupied by the energetic youngsters who would come by later.

The grass was sparkling with traces of heavy dew, promising a nice day.

'At last after prolonged rains, nature will revive, ready to welcome summer,' he was saying to himself.

He thought that avocado should learn a few facts about nature and the seasons. Tropical plants were not aware of the phenomena of the Northern hemisphere because their genes were programmed differently.

He began his talk with Caesar by explaining about the plantain tree under which they were sitting. To make the avocado be attentive, he turned it around and pulled the branches up.

"This is a plantain; it takes its origin in the South like you. Every autumn it loses its leaves and sheds its bark, leaving the trunk bare and white."

He kept on turning the plant to make it easier to see the inhabitants of the park and get acquainted with them.

Behind their bench there were lilac bushes and still further stood azalea and rhododendrons, ready to bloom.

"Very soon all of them will be covered with bright flowers, changing the whole vista into a new enchanting world. It will be beautiful. When autumn arrives, leaves on many trees will turn yellow - except for conifers, which you can see on the hill. But this will be for the next time."

Such excursions soon became the norm and every Sunday Nick told the avocado more facts about the vegetal world, pulling out of his memory long forgotten terminology and explanations.

A the start, he felt embarrassed being seen in the park with a plant in his hands. But soon he realized that other visitors' behavior also could not be explained from any reasonable point of view and he stopped being shy. Besides characters that came there to split a bottle and smoke a joint, older women walked their cats, giving them a chance to hear birds. There was also a small crowd of men who arrived in the afternoon and installed themselves at the basketball court. They watched the youngsters silently and then were gone.

Nobody paid attention to Nick. He carefully put the pot with the plant next to him, sat down and started enjoying himself.

'Look here,' he said, turning the avocado to the right. 'On the slope you can see a very beautiful tree. It is called a Cedar of Lebanon. It originated in the same part of the world as you and I believe you can become friends. But you should be careful, because it is wild and unruly, while you came from a greenhouse. You are tender and fragile."

Nck was certain the avocado was wholly enchanted by his explanations. He was a born educationalist and nothing brought him more pleasure than to lecture others and make them absorb his knowledge, even if his pupil was a plant.

Over the next few months, the avocado continued to grow. Its leaves were wide, the branches elongated, and the only thing which made Nick sad was that it did not bear fruit. He did not know how to make it fertile.

Once sitting on his favorite bench, Nick said aloud that he would like to take the plant to the South and put it somewhere on the shores of the Mediterranean sea, either the European side or African, in Italy or Morocco. Then he fell silent, wondering what had happened to him and why he made such a promise.

'Good that Caesar does not understand my words. Otherwise, I would feel awkward.'

But he was carried away by his dreams. He envisioned delightful pictures of being there in the South with the avocado plant, meeting the sun daily and traveling together with it through the day towards the sunset. The avocado would be below his window in the garden. Under his protection, it would turn into a mature tree with abundant foliage and heavy fruit hanging from its branches.

Life continued. The damp spring and rainy summer were replaced by a mild autumn, lit by timid sunrays.

But one day a conflict developed. Nick had a girlfriend who frequented him and sometimes stayed for a couple of days. She was cheerful and kind, and Nick liked her company. They developed a close relationship, trusting each other with small secrets and hopes. She was curious and noticing the avocado, asking him about its origin.

Listening to Nick's story, she got interested and sometimes even tried to take care of it. But Nick observed that with her arrival something strange was happening to the plant. It was as if her presence deprived it of its joie de vivre. The leaves began losing their luster and the branches had a hard time maintaining their posture. He could not discern the silent appeal that touched him at the beginning of their life together.

For a while, he preferred to ignore the signs. But when they occurred regularly, he could not overlook the obvious and had to reflect.

Clearly, the plant was not pleased by his relationship with the girl, no matter how hard he wanted to close his eyes to this fact, not wishing to disturb his romance. As soon as the girlfriend arrived, the plant folded its leaves and did not open them till the woman was gone. As usual, the woman saw nothing ...up to a point.

If the lady was absent for a few days, the plant's leaves opened up, the shine returned and Nick felt invisible vibrations from it getting to him. The mood of the plant could be described as victorious. Nicholas detected the sort of ambiance reigning at military parades when uniformed soldiers marched behind a band ready to advance on an invisible enemy.

He knew that Caesar was jealous and made it a rule to move the plant when the lady was in his apartment from the bedroom to the living room.

This gesture did not help much. Feeling her presence, the plant withered and Nick worried about its wellbeing. Even the young and vigorous baby leaves looked sad. No matter what Nick was attempting, like watering, dusting it, polishing its trunk, the plant suffered.

One evening the inevitable happened. As Nick has guessed correctly, the lady felt neglected and became offended by his indifference. Though he did not demonstrate his excessive attention to the plant, the lady could not help wondering why it received such care. The strain became still more obvious after he declined her offer to spend a weekend at the seashore. She knew he had nothing particular to do and nevertheless said to her that he could not be out of town on Sunday.

He was sitting on a sofa and clogged his ears, trying not to listen to her screaming,

"What have you found in this plant? A friend? A relative? This pile of miserable leaves is dearer to you than I? Are you eager to replace me with that? I feel sorry for you. My deepest regret is that I did not find out earlier that you are in need of serious treatment, with your attitude to life and people.

"What do you see in that plant? I'll tell you what I see- a bundle of miserable twigs. If they last another week, I will be amazed. I should have learned earlier that you have no human feeling left, that everything was absorbed by that ephemeral shrub. If someone finds out about that, you will end up in an asylum. I believed we had a normal, agreeable relationship and instead I see that your folly went beyond all restraints and borders, that you are ready to replace me with a pile of half dead roots. I won't be surprised if next week you will be borne in a funeral procession with a band and mourners."

Nick was deeply offended and finally could not stay silent: "Why do you say that? To get me upset? The avocado is in a very good, healthy shape. In three months, it did not lose a single leaf and added three more."

She laughed hysterically and kept on staring at Nick in disbelief. Her eyes were getting bigger and bigger. She tried to say something but could not because of overwhelming emotions. Finally, she waved her hand and left the apartment.

Before closing the door, she issued an ultimatum: "You have to choose. It will be either me or that item."

There was the rhythmic clicking of her heels along new tiles as she left the house. It got quieter and quieter, finally everything went still. Nick sank to the floor: "What shall I do?"

He gazed at the avocado. His anger was rising.

"What are you doing to me? Do you want to get me entirely under your power? Is it what you want? Is that it? It won't happen. Never!" He furiously grabbed the thin trunk and held it tightly.

'I love you, take care of you, but you want more? What right do you have to deprive me of my joy? I know, you don't want to have rivals even though there is no danger to your existence. Why do you do that? It is not honest and not right. The same old story repeats itself and you are not better than others. You think only about yourself and not about me, me who do everything for you and even quarreled with my girlfriend.

'I guess you can't behave otherwise. I was telling you about the trees and did not say a word about our civilization. We all are fighting for the place of number one, for the chance to be on top and have others obey our orders. Judging by your behavior, I realize that it does not matter what kind of species we are. Everyone behaves the same."

What happened next was unclear. Nick awoke in the middle of the night, when a strange voice was talking, "Et tu, Brutus!"

In the morning, everything was as usual, except for one peculiarity. The avocado was not in the living room, but in his bedroom and he could not figure out when he had moved it.

The plant raised its branches. They were reaching out for him, filled with love and tenderness. His animosity disappeared.

He whispered: "I promise to accept only a woman who will love you."

Still under the strain of his promise he tiptoed to the front door and went to the bar. After having two beers, he relaxed and could judge the situation with a cool head.

'Let's admit that my behavior is peculiar, at least in the eyes of normal people. But normal people of my age have families, unlike me. They are not lonely. I don't want to have a cat or a dog. This plant suits me perfectly, the same as my lady. I like her humor and optimism, two things missing from my character.'

The more he thought about her, the more he regretted the quarrel. 'She is my sunray in this gloomy town.'

Reproaches to the avocado were on the tip of his tongue and ready to pour out, but he stopped in time, remembering that the plant had no feet and could not run down the stairs. Instead of making a scene similar to what his girlfriend had done, he decided to speak to it.

His anger was gone. He was thinking: 'It looks like I lost my girlfriend and now I can lose my close friend. It would be prudent to explain things to Caesar. The plant is not aware of many things and it is my obligation to teach it.'

'Women are dangerous and powerful,' he began. 'They look feeble, but that impression is deceptive. We love their soft and tender embraces, but their soft paws circle us in hoops of iron. You grew up in a hot house where the rules are different and you exist on your own vegetal level. In a hot house, everything is simpler, because nobody will let you fight each other and you can only bark at your neighbors from a distance, not able to break someone's neck, as we, the humans do. In our life, there is a permanent war between everybody and with everybody, sometimes hidden and sometimes exposed. Our existence knows no peace treaties, only temporary armistices and women are particularly vengeful and intolerant. Don't hope to get compassion from them. But I confess to you that without their company life is not worth living. Look at my lady. She left in tantrum, but she knows that victory was hers and I will crawl back to her."

That night his sleep was anguished, with a sequence of fleeting, scary and ill-defined dreams. He fancied himself a child surrounded by a crowd of monstrous aggressive strangers. He was alone and nobody could come to his rescue.

'Mommy, mommy, where are you?'

His own sobs awoke him. Still under the impression of some big hands reaching out for him, he sat on the bed, trying to comprehend where he was. The same strange toneless voice not belonging to a human asked, "When are we leaving for the Cote d'Azur?"

He jumped out of the bed, realizing that the nightmare was gone and he was back in his room surrounded by familiar things.

Putting his head on the pillow and drowsing, he noticed blue leaves suddenly growing in size and reaching enormous proportions. Soon his vision was blocked by bright blue foliage which did not let in a crack for anything else.

'Is it the avocado?' he asked himself in panic. 'This is something else and this giant scares me.' He shrieked.

Under dim light coming from outside lanterns, a silhouette of the avocado was reflected on the wall of his bedroom, while the plant itself remained in the shade. Nick walked over to it and saw it was tranquil and sleeping. By now he had learned to divine its mood and by the state of the leaves, he understood the plant could not be the cause of alarm.

He retired to bed and tried to fall asleep again. But no matter what he did, sleep did not come. Herbal tea, a sleeping pill, massaging his heels –nothing worked and he stayed wide-awake.

Staring at the ceiling, he counted elephants, an old artifice, hoping that the monotonous chant would help, while a tender caress passed along his body. His skin revived and every pore opened up, absorbing the pleasure. The needles prickling his heels and causing his insomnia disappeared as he heard an enjoyable sweet melody, enchanting and captivating, but so quiet that he struggled to hear it. His eyes closed without any effort, even if he attempted to stay awake to hear more. He turned, touched the avocado's elongated trunk and fell asleep with a smile on his lips.

The next morning, he woke up relaxed and well rested. The night's bad dreams evaporated from his brain as if they had never existed. Even the quarrel looked like a trifle and he knew that things would straighten out.

It was Sunday. Not wishing to lose time, he was getting ready for his usual walk in the park.

Just as he was standing on the threshold of his apartment holding the plant in one hand and closing the door with the other, his girlfriend came walking up. She was smiling and holding her hands back as if she was hiding something.

"Can I go with you?' she asked.

Not showing his surprise, Nick nodded his assent. At that moment, she took out from behind her back a plant. It was a young avocado.

Nick's Present - A story in the spirit of *The Bonfire of Vanities*

This year the writers' retreat sessions started as usual. Would-be celebrity writers gathered at the Siddhartha Buddhist retreat located 40 km from Brussels in the provincial depths of Flanders.

Buddhist retreat, you may wonder….To be sure, these Westerners have nothing in common with Buddhists. It is improbable that any of them ever entered golden-domed temples and prostrated themselves at the base of huge smiling benevolent figures, or put wooden sticks of different lengths in a porcelain vessel and, after mixing them for a few moments while keeping their eyes closed, pulled out the longest one and made a wish, then burned it in a flat oval chalice and went home appeased, leaving behind golden idols with everlasting smiles.

No, they were not into that. These eighteen middle aged men and women of predominantly Anglo-Saxon origin came here to spend three days learning the secrets of successfully knitting together words and turning them into bestsellers.

They had chosen the Flemish town Tremolo thanks to its proximity to Brussels, where they all resided at the time. The Siddhartha offered tranquility and a very reasonable rental fee for a long weekend.

Not to waste precious time, on the way to Tremolo they stopped at a supermarket and picked up an ample amount of booze to keep them going for three days.

Nick Hogg was a leader. His age, grayish hair and impressive stature allowed him to assume that position. His height was above average and he had wide shoulders and a powerful anatomy. His massive head was set on a short, strong neck. His facial features were basic. That and its bronzed color reminded you of one of Picasso's cubist portraits.

Nick took charge of the organization of this year's retreat, including setting the bonfire at the end of the last session. His vision was to present his surprise after the closing ceremony. Nobody was aware of that, not a soul.

The sessions went smoothly, similar to previous years. Aspiring writers were hard at work, constructing dialogues, doing characterization pieces, describing their inner dreams and secret thoughts. Several women even composed poems and were applauded by other members. They all encouraged one another, and even when a piece of prose was mediocre and met with prolonged silence, the awkward pause was quickly dissipated by hesitant exclamations and encouraging smiles. Comedy sketches were staged to the enjoyment of actors and audience.

The last day seemed routine, as well, and no one paid attention to Nick's two-hour absence.

When the writers came out of their session, happy, excited, liberated, leaving behind the conference room, they felt as if they were taken by boat away from Monte Cristo's Chateau d'If, away from the dungeons and heading for sunny Marseilles.

After a hard day's work, everyone was hungry and ready to sample the wine waiting on the table next to the window in the main parlor. The evening continued with more stories told mixed with anecdotes. People were waiting for dinner to be prepared and set, but even though it was taking longer than usual, no one complained.

Everyone was at ease, except for Nick. He had been plotting something extraordinary never seen and done before and he was quite nervous and restless.

From time to time, he came out and looked at the sky, not trusting the weather channel's indication of a beautiful sunset. But the sky showed no traces of clouds or possible rain and he calmed down.

This year was a turning point in his generally smooth life. He was leaving Brussels and the writer's group and he needed to do something to leave a mark, something that people would remember him by.

After the stock of bottles on the table was drawn down sharply and the battery of empty bottles under the table reached substantial proportions, the noise level in the room grew so powerful that when Nick rose and attempted to make a statement, nobody could hear him. But finally all eyes turned towards him and he delivered his long awaited statement that "Supper is ready". Making welcoming gestures, he invited the participants to proceed outside.

As the group exited, at first they did not notice anything unusual. The familiar well-groomed green lawn stretched out in front of the building, its monotony interrupted by clusters of bushes and benches set around flower beds. The writers looked, squinting after the somber light of the conference room. Further on they saw an assortment of benches grouped around wooden tables and a pyramid of logs, skewers over them, fixed on metal supports drilled into stones.

"Barbecue!" Norton exclaimed, and was surprised to meet a sarcastic look from Nick. But in the next moment this look changed into a jovial smile, which lit Nick's face, cutting his age by ten years.

"You will see," he replied enigmatically, approaching the construction. Yes, it looked like a barbecue, and its smoldering stones betrayed its age and frequent use.

Nick started the fire, which quickly spread and enveloped the dry logs.

Soon people gathered around, holding out their plates on which generous amount of chicken parts, lamb ribs, sausages, potatoes and onion rings were loaded.

After the tables were cleaned and the dishes put away, Nick rose and began his little speech: "I hope you have followed my suggestion and brought along your main projects, what you have been working at during the last few months."

A chorus of content and happy people responded, "Yes, Yes."

"Could you show me these hard copies? I ask all of you to put them in front of you on the table".

Bewildered, the authors obeyed, some hesitantly, some frowning, as they started to suspect something.

Soon an ample pile of white paper sheets grew and was visible on each table.

Larisa mumbled, "I wondered why we were asked to bring our stories if they were not used during the sessions. Are we going to work now?"

Nick smiled enigmatically, "Larisa, be patient and you will find out."

Noticing an inquiring look on Jack's face, ready to lift his hand, he shot at him, "Hold your horses. Don't rush. Everything comes in time."

Glancing at the table where white sheets formed a tall and neat pile in front of Norton, he nodded approvingly, "You have worked zealously and produced a lot. This snow white stack is the proof of your talent. Look at this collection, all of you, and appreciate what Norton had achieved."

Some people stirred nervously, trying to hide their jealousy. Larisa felt crestfallen, touching her meager 20 sheets of unfinished stories and poems in need of correction. Not much to boast about. She threw a glance at beaming Norton. Someone was patting her on the shoulder. Sara was looking at her reassuringly, pointing to the very thin pile sitting in front of her. Not more than ten pages. She probably wanted to comfort Larisa, saying, "You are not the only one." Anyway, her support was welcome.

Nick continued: "Now I want to say a few words about Yaroslav. He can be another lesson to all of you. Soon Yaroslav will complete his historic novel, a few hundred pages of it. He works harder than others and it is fair that this novel is coming to its conclusion".

"David's hero', - Nick touched the pile of papers in front of David, - 'in two weeks will discover Y. That will be another victory for the fighting spirit of this great group. I've picked up the best examples and omitted those who are not a credit to the group. Having this in mind and thinking how to stir your imagination, I've come to the conclusion that something drastic has to be done. Now all of you listen to me attentively, very attentively."

He did not need to insist on the last demand. Every member of the group straightened himself up and watched Nick.

"To liberate your creative spirit, your energy, your libido, I suggest we empty the brain from old burdens, make it free and receptive to new ideas, new winds of creation, and new waves of spatial energy. How do we do that? Very simply. Here we have our sacred creations, aspirations and hopes. They will all turn to ashes, will be purified by fire and will set you free. It was taking too long for you to complete your projects. Except for three of you, nobody was inspired and you all were dragging your feet. The only solution is to help you. I am doing it for you. Get free your spirit, get free!"

Chanting, he picked up piles of paper sheets of 'In Search of Y' one by one and threw them into the fire, which by that time had spread deep and wide. The flame was rising higher and higher.

The writers screamed, jumped to their feet, some even made attempts to save their stories from the fire. That was until they heard David's calm voice: "Surely, we can recover everything from our hard disks."

But, in response, Nick was laughing." Ha, Ha, Ha."

"What is gone is gone. You are free. But I promise to you that from now on you will be writing as fast as your fingers can type."

People listened, trying to understand where Nick was leading them. Meanwhile, he came to the table where Norton was seated, lifted a page and tossed it into the fire. It happened to be the opening page of Nortons's story about God.

Norton jumped to his feet, unprepared for such a development. But in his astonishment he could not say a word. Instead he was stuttering. "Bb, Bb, Bb."

Nick laughed and flung several more sheets into the fire before John grabbed his hands.

Larisa watched Nick with a smile and felt something else was going to happen, but what? What will be his next trick?

As if answering her question, Nick put his disheveled hair in order, smoothed the collar of his blue shirt which John had torn and said calmly, "It is not as simple as you think. Better follow my advice and start a new thing. You will be amazed how fast you will complete it."

The fire was roaring on, just as he had hoped. A triumphant smile lit Nick's face and did not leave it. "The deed is done. All you'll have to do is to watch."

His voice had an ominous tone, but he was overtaken by the exclamations of the onlookers. They were staring in awe at the space above the burning logs. The rising smoke played bizarre pranks, creating the apparitions of the characters conceived by the authors.

Norton was the first to jump up when he saw Mr. Nice grabbing God by the neck. The eyes of Mr. Nice betrayed fury. A fleeing thought passed through Norton's head. 'If I were God, I would be scared for my life, even in my eternal living state'.

"Not that!" - He shouted. "I never wanted them to fight. You should have listened when I read my sequence".

"Shhhh!" Nick whispered. 'Watch!"

Two figures tied up in their eternal embrace were floating higher and higher noiselessly, silently. Mr. Nice's hands were still squeezing God's neck. The whole scene resembled a sequence from a silent movie. Even the bursts of fire and sizzling of logs fell quiet.

David was holding his both hands firmly on the table, fearing he would fly off and not wanting to do that. Jen Zo and Qlifah, both in unbelievable attire, which could not be found in any corner of Earth, circled the area around the green lawn before they departed to the place from where there was no return. David dropped his head, refusing to face the reproachful gazes of his creations. He knew they had something for which to reprimand him and did not want to hear that. He remained bent down, with his eyes closed, until he heard Derek's voice, "Johnny, stay put, don't leave your basement." Everyone was watching how Johnny crawled out of the basement window and hurried after a pair of beautiful muscular legs. "Johnny," groaned Derek and closed his eyes in despair. "I am sorry, Johnny. I did not mean that."

The apparitions were gone. The residue of smoke filled the evening air. Everything was still, when suddenly an unexpected movement started at the level of the fire. Now smoke was forming waves, which were getting bigger and more powerful and ominous. Between them, a fragile sailboat was struggling to move forward. It seemed to be abandoned when suddenly the smoke made a twist and out of obscurity a thin figure emerged. He was alone.

Robert recognized his creation, and shouted, unable to restrain his fear. "Alfred! Help him. It is your son, Alexander!"

Alongside the boat, an older woman with long black hair appeared. She was growing bigger than the boat, bigger than the sails. She stretched out her arms, which became longer than the height of the sails, and pulled the boy from the edge of the sea.

Robert was sitting still. Big drops of sweat were forming on his forehead. His cheeks were wet, but he did not bother to wipe them. "Thank you, Ya Ya, thank you!" he exclaimed. "This is exactly the image I had formed in my head. You are precious!"

Nick lifted his arms, "Now it is my turn. My novel is a sequence of long and sometimes too detailed pieces. But I love my characters and want to present them to you. They are here at your disposal."

Abashed, the audience watched a complicated picture forming in front of their eyes, as if painted by a magical brush. Only now it was created by smoke. The lianas, the rocks, the palm trees, the wet forest. They all filled in the air, as if Chronos turned back the time and brought from oblivion the magic lantern, the invention of former centuries.

Since not everyone attended Thursday sessions and did not penetrate the adventures of African characters conceived by Nick, they watched the picture with curiosity, but without emotional involvement. They did not know the peregrinations of Nick's characters in dangerous surroundings. The main character, Tennyson, was struggling with his past and his future. The first he was trying to forget, the second to postpone. One more person appeared, Pink Sister Jacky. They were involved in a dispute, and the complicated *tableau vivant* kept on changing according to the characters' words. The persons fought, argued, kissed and loved each other. They were becoming many, including soldiers, missionaries, and pedestrians in big African cities. The writers did not expect Nick could follow the plot development, but everyone felt the tension and did not dare to look at Nick.

"I don't understand,' he commented. 'You were not supposed to be here. Go away."

He waved his hands, trying to send the smoke in another direction. But the apparitions formed a close knot and went up just above his head, suspended like a balloon.

"Stop it, Nick!' Sarah screamed. 'Enough is enough!"

Nick's sarcastic smile turned malicious. "Bear it just a bit longer, Sarah, and you will understand everything."

While people were gasping, stunned, still refusing to believe what they had witnessed, clever and pragmatic David got up from the table. 'Big Deal,' he said. "I will take my computer and show to them that Nick is a shrink. He has deceived us. Besides, why should we lose our stories? I worked hard, the others as well. I will find the file 'In Search of Y' and show it to Nick. Imagine his sour face when I cite the first sentence from the introduction.'

Still murmuring, he reached his room, found his PC and returned to the lawn. Turning on the computer and listening to its familiar branded start melody, he jubilantly said: "Thank you, Nick. I appreciate your attempt to free our brains. It was a brilliant idea. Now watch me." He took in all the authors with his eyes, feeling a wave of pride and triumph rising inside. "I will prove to you that if we want to revive our stories and continue working at them till they are finished, we can do it."

He cast a glance at the screen and frowned. Something was not right. The screen was empty. Feverishly he pushed buttons, checked the connections, shook the machine, lifted it and checked the back. But the screen was dark and silent.

"I don't get it,' he began, searching for Nick and stopped short. Across him at the other side of the table, where a minute ago solid Nick's figure occupied the place, he was staring at an empty chair.

'Really, where is Nick?" In the sudden silence, Ann's voice sent resonant waves around the table. Everyone seemed to be asking the same question. "Surely, he is around. I saw him a minute ago."

David leaned towards Norton. "Could you bring your computer? Let's see what has happened to your story."

"Why?" Norton replied. 'I committed myself to turn a new page and I am doing it."

Kathleen got up: "I will get mine." She left, but slowly the residue of the event was settling in. They all suspected the truth. It was a strange magical act, and Nick had succeeded in performing it. How and why, nobody could say. But one thing was obvious: he had expunged their stories, thus forcing them to do new things.

Norton was talking. "After all, this is not a bad idea. Look at Larisa, she sits with her village story much too long. I can say the same about Yaroslav. How many more years do we have to follow the adventures of his lovers? They are not yet lovers after several hundred pages. I welcome your next novel, Yaroslav."

The fire was still licking at burned, darkened logs. Rare sparkles shot up and disappeared in the transparent and fragrant air. Time was moving towards midnight and the universe was set to sleep.

"I offer a toast to the bonfire of vanities,' Norton said. 'They will burn and from their ashes new ideas will emerge, more brilliant and talented. To us all."

Silence descended and nobody rushed to pick up the ashes of their magical stories which were still smoldering.

Crucifixion Flower

The day was long
Centuries long,
Oval shaped, oblong
It had original weight,
Sodden with loss and hate.
Born from sapping pain
Christian salvation slowly came,
But His life, that charitable foundation
Was wasted.
It was doomed salvation.
Centuries long day, perturbed,
Smelt of death, love drained.
Jerusalem, crusaders' shame
Destroyed, bronze based pain.
Alone, man plays
With days of toys
Oval shaped.
His naïve joys
Return to hate and
Sodden dross.

Autumn-Flower

Autumn, bare branches...

When evening casts the shade of darkness
Across my wet and foggy window
Obscure and unwelcome figures
Are swaying under cobwebs in the corners.

That overwhelming voice of silence,
As deep as thunderous bells of Easter service,
More resonant than villain's basso in the final act.
As frightful as the hidden breathing of the caves.

I strain my ears. Do I hear the mouse's scratching?
Or the idle humming of the fly?
The delicate mosquito's lie?
I recognize the squeaking whisper of the bats.
The planks are moving and the figures in the corners
Are stirring on their knees.
Their blinded eyes are looking into space.

That ominous sensation. My loneliness.
That gloomy hour and no help in sight.
I know I shall never catch the firebird.
That luck is never mine.
The tide is coming and the tide is going,
The firebird is nesting on the Nile.

Oh, that confusing human fate
Encircled by the strings of cobweb.
Another moment, and another...my candle is dying.

The darkness swallows the reddish light.
The waxen liquid tears have no might
To break the silky threads still sticking to my palms.

The flame is losing height.
The moon is hidden by the branches of midnight.
It carries no peace and no answers.

Oh, that torturous evening. Whom should I blame?
The night? The silence of the phone? The rain?
They all combine and challenge me.
As I retreat I count precious time
And hold the candle in my hands
The flame of which absorbs my lifeless fingers.
....
Autumn, bare branches and the crimson blossoms of
geraniums
Reflected in the melted depth of life...

Reflections

Reflections in a hospital ward
The day is running like a deer chased by a Russian hound
Whose deep-throated howl is fading in the coming dusk.
The pigeons are flying slowly, their heavy bodies
Lag hopelessly behind the sunset that glides by
My window encircled by the universe.
I feel like following them too, wishing to give up the
Loneliness and clarity of the inescapable night.
Down on the road I see the cars compete against red lights.
Big and sparkling letters spell the destiny for each.

They never see it, they are blind.
Casual spectator, a Russian doll with bound limbs,
I envy human haste in which I can't take part.
I long for company, for human voices.
Two halves of me, identical to a stranger's eyes strive for
Contrasting values. One says: Dash down,
Stop flying in the clouds and join the stream of cars.
You will forget the pain, the time, the years.
These deceptive words fill my soul with hope alike
The wind that rises and foretells a
Coming tide submerging the coastal trails.
To obey the impulse will give me pleasure
For a moment. But later on, my eyes will turn to
Crystal air with a question: Shall I be here
Excluded from the frantic life below?
The other part of me stays still.
Streams of clouds pass in the evening
Purple sky. They say: What can be better than to
Jump and grasp a shapeless cloud by the tail and, slowly
Dissolving into water, fall like welcome rain
Onto newborn sprouts?
Eternity is here. It has been reached.

I am losing hope of finding proper balance
Between the somber and the brighter parts
Of the entire undivided spirit. My unavailing efforts make
The ceiling darker. I cannot! My destiny is here! Am I still alive?
Is that not the most important thing in life?
To guess the sense of Belshazzar's letters
And mark the route accordingly? Ignore the obstacles!
The soul traverses them as if they were
The birch tree shadows that cross the

Forest paths in glittering summer heat.
But the longings of obscure nature keep us prisoner
And quitting, leave us barren. My dreams are
Rich in images, but my desires are humble. As night
Descends, my room becomes a tower
Suspended from the stars, I tell my limbs,
Unwilling to obey the words: Trust me. The magic motions
Are here, just obscured by the ruffled waters. As if
The kingdom by the sea were not submerged by
Envious Niadas. Its vision is here,
Reflected in the air above the shallow bay.
You look inside the wave, you see the castle.
The sea retreats, the castle will remain.

The pigeons disperse, retreating for the night.
Shall I overcome remorse?
Or try to find the proper scriptures on the wall?
Or with my eager heart attempt to join my feathery
companions
Assembled for the night in their nests of stone?
I fall asleep. I dream. The storm is calming down.
Hope is slowly reviving as the Vesuvius ashes avenge my
tower
And I walk out freely.

August

The roses sunbathe
Their smiles grow wider
As old sol approaches its midday apogee.

An ominous and weighty cloud impregnated
With tons of ice and water floats above uncertain
Where to discharge its burden

Pigeon-egg hailstones will be shooting in a moment.
Colors, life and breath are gone, the petals will fall off
Dark and shrunken as tender quails
Left breathless by a skillful hunter
Now waiting on the surface of a lake
To be collected by a frantic, merciless setter.

But still the fragrant petals are alive and full of bloom.
Still the shadows they cast are pink and white and crimson.
Still the humming birds are busy sucking sweet perfume
With elongated beaks sheltered in the plume.

Who can divine the sense of this fragmented universe?
Composed of magic colors, crystal sounds and rotting
bodies?
Who wants to sacrifice his idle muse
To grasp the sense of mystery concealed in morning fog?
Who can commit himself to undertake the work of Sisyphus
And shift obediently the fallen rocks
To find one sacred word, defining the creation of the world?

We dread the future
We avoid the fortune tellers
We keep on walking towards obscurity
Persuaded that in some other garden, other time,
And at some distant planet
We shall do better.

Orpheus

The trees grow no leaves for fear
Of hindering the tune,
The ants stop scaling dunes;
Forgotten, their hungry queen,
The song is reigning.

Hypnotized, the birds are circling,
Recounting the melody.
The lions have disguised their nails,
A hint of smile on their bushy faces,
The song is reigning.

Orpheus sings. His crystal melody reflects
The starry night above the ancient Knossos palace.
Blue acrobats are flying
On frescoed walls,
Escaping the abusive horns.
The Minotaur has lost its throne.

My virgin wife, you've gone.
I cry and groan.
I turn to stone.
The world enclosing me is furious.
I am left alone surrounded by shrieking furies.

The melody is lost in shadows.
My lyre breaks
And no hope remains.
The splinters plummet to the sea.
The waves conceal the strings.

Silence reigns.

Orpheus, your golden lyre reveres Euridice.
Her tragic death brought no end to your ardent love.
Delays and doubts did not crawl like worms in your noble heart.
Who else among the mortals would cross the river Styx
And be rewarded with Persephone's tender smile?
Who would sustain
The heavy menace of Pluto's gaze without fleeing for exile?
Who else remained alive without bending down
Under the weight of piercing sounds?
We, Euridice's sisters,
Look in vain
For the daring image of Orpheus,
Consumed by melancholy shadows.
Silence reigns.

Phaedra

Turquoise, sapphire, cobalt blue
Your shining eyes are two lagoons
Gauged through the surface of the land.
Or maybe, this is Neptune's gaze.
The God is guarding his domain.

You stare at my face,
The silence reigns.
The question forms
What is behind my tense
And awkward smile.

I dare not to raise
My head.
I feel, I guess, I know
Your mane of shiny hair
Shields me
From distress.

Yesterday I saw you riding horses
You make Apollo- the god of Sun morose
The way you hold the reins
Of that gilded chariot.

I watched Olympic Games,
In the crowd of the peasant boys
You stood out
All naked, lovely
As the Praxitel marble.
When the race began
Excitement went to your sex
And then I lost you.
The sunrays blinded me
Annoyed that I adore your grace.

It is getting dark, the servant girls are singing,
The lonely Shepard summons goats to go home.
The purple roof of Knossos palace burns
As if engulfed by flame.

The evening meals unite the families.
For me the torture just begins.
To face my husband, servants, guests
To dance and to receive the compliments.

To sit across from you
Absorbed in my chagrin
When my heart is pained,
Pierced by the needles.
To raise a goblet to my lips
And taste the poison.

But what comes next-
Still worse,
My husband's clumsy lust.
I close my eyes.
In my delirium I think-
It's you, not him inside my womb.
I call him Hippolytus - he laughs.
I scream.

At last Aurora passes through
The morning air.
I stare at the golden glare.
The day begins.

And you appear glorious, refreshed, accompanied
By humming bees.

One word, one glance, one smile
You will transform the world of Phaedra.
The melody of treasured dream will never die
The hope is singing in my ear.

About the Brussels Writers Circle

THE BRUSSELS WRITERS' CIRCLE meets every Tuesday night from 7pm, every Thursday night from 7pm. The group is open to anyone with an interest in writing, and writers of all genres are welcome. In addition to its twice weekly meetings, it also organises a twice yearly writing retreat in the Flemish countryside open to both members and non-members.

Founded in 1997, the group has now almost 200 members of all nationalities. Although the group meets and discusses works in English, it is open to both mother and non-mother tongue speakers and is indeed proud to count members from Spain, Italy, Sweden, Finland, the Seychelles, Zimbabwe and many many more...

As we like to say:

Welcome –Bienvenue –Welkom –Bienvenidos – Wilkommen – Croeso – Benvenuto!

Author Bios

Jaroslav Albert was born in Slovakia. At age sixteen he moved to the United States. After high school, he entered the City University of New York, where he studied classical painting and sculpture. Later he became interested in the sciences and went on to obtain a graduate degree in physics. He started reading fiction at age twenty-four and first tried his hand at writing fiction at thirty. He prefers writing novels in which cliché, and often seedy characters turn into cliché-defying (anti)heroes.

 jaroslavalbert81@gmail.com

T. D. Arkenberg is a writer of contemporary stories. Characters that pop off the page, vivid descriptions and crisp dialogue characterize his work. He has an MBA from The University of Chicago and a BA in Literature from Northwestern University. T.D. has published two novels, Final Descent (Outskirts Press, 2013) and, JELL-O and Jackie O (Outskirts Press 2014). A third novel, None Shall Sleep a tale of perseverance set in Italy and London, is planned for a late 2015 release. He's currently at work on a memoir, Two Towers, focusing on his executive role at United Airlines during the tragic events of September 11, and the simultaneous deaths of his parents. www.TDArkenberg.com

C.S. Begu is a Romanian, born behind the Iron Curtain. He grew up by the Mountain, then 22 years later he moved across the Ocean, then moved back from across the Ocean, then married childhood friend, and now he's raising junior in the land of the Little Boy Who Pees. Meanwhile, he wrote the short pieces that you just read. You like? Then write to csbegu@gmail.com. And, while you're surfing the Internet, help the writers in this book out by writing a review on Amazon. Thank you.

Simon Boylan was born in 1979 in Dublin, Ireland. He is a jack of all trades and so far, master of none. He has lived in Brussels since the summer of 2010 and is still working on his first novel. He hopes to finish it before the world ends.

Alex Dampney has written a number of short stories, but prefers the discipline of poetry. She also paints in oils and finds the two practices, which both use images and metaphor, to express complex emotions and experiences, complement each other. She started writing about 10 years ago, when she was forty. alex.dampney@gmail.com

Claire Davenport is a journalist and writer based in Brussels. Her favourite authors are Siri Hustvedt and Zadie Smith and in her spare time she runs, paints, cooks, goes for long walks and mooches around the house drinking tea.

Gerrit De Feyter, educated in Ghent, left Belgium aged 22. 8 years abroad across 6 countries followed. This experience shaped his opinions and personality. Having Asperger Syndrome, OCD, and high-sensitivity, Gerrit started writing and performing poetry as "Illusion of Purity", to raise awareness on these issues and fight its taboos. http://thepathslesstravelled.wordpress.com http://www.ill usionofpurity.com

Larisa Doctorow (Zalesova) is a journalist and a critic. Doctorow's articles in English have been published in The Wall Street Journal, The Bulletin, The Russia Journal and The St Petersburg Times. Her articles on musical life and the arts first appeared in Russian language publications in 1994 in leading newspapers and magazines of Moscow and St Petersburg. Since that time she has been a correspondent of the Paris-based language weekly La Pensée Russe and of the Radio Corporation of St Petersburg. In 1998 the periodical Zvezda in St Petersburg named her the winner of an annual prize for her artistic achievements. Her novel *Live as Before* was published in 2012 in St Petersburg. She lives in Brussels and in St Petersburg. zalesova@yahoo.com

Based in Brussels for over 20 years, **Kevin Dwyer** is a native of Boston, Massachusetts and writes short stories, film scripts and lyrics, as well as scholarly articles. His recent writing, both fiction and non-fiction, has focussed on various aspects of food and eating, and he is currently writing a speculative novel which takes place in an ultra-thin near future. His short story, *Candy*, was adapted into a short subject in 2003. kdwyer@skynet.be

David Ellard is originally from London but lived in Brussels for twenty years. He has been active in the Brussels Writers' Circle since the century began and has now written the first draft of an epic science fiction novel, a surrealist-erotic short story, a 'lad-lit' short story and is working on various projects in various forms and genres: short story, novella, sci-fi, fantasy, young adult, not forgetting an existential Buddhist murder story.

Sarah R. Harris: Some of her children's books are translated into Dutch and have been the subject of various educational projects, both in Belgium and in Scotland. She organizes poetry workshops and teaches English to refugees. She is now working on an adult novel which has something to do with … cows! I Isle of Skye www.asheepcalledskye.com

Nick Hogg, NLP Practioner/Coach | Advanced English Lessons Online, Public Relations and Communications, University of Turin, Cambridge College, Highgate School, London.

Kevin Ireland is one of New Zealand's most prominent and well-loved writers and has published 18 collections of poetry since 1963, as well as a collection of short stories and 6 novels. Kevin has won numerous awards, including the 2004 Prime Minister's Award for Literary Achievement. The fun of art is from his 2012 collection Dreamy days and nothing done.

Barbara Koethe loves to look around and loves to listen. Sometimes the pictures she sees and the words she hears take her to a story. And sometimes she writes it down. That's fun. She is from Cologne and happens to be a member in the Swansea and the Brussels Writing Circle.

Nathan E. Johnson: Writer, Director, Wacky on the Junk Serial Deletion Editor, Utah Film & Media Guild* Member/WRITER (*maybe not the name but probably), retired from the USAF after 24 years and currently working and studying film & media production in northern Utah. His previous duty stations include Berlin, Germany, Mildenhall,

UK, the Presidio of Monterey, California, Anjeong-ri, Republic of Korea, and Brussels, Belgium. More of his work can be found at
http://astronautrockstar.squarespace.com
novecho@hotmail.com

Martin R. Jones was born in England and has lived in Brussels for almost 20 years. He writes short stories, novellas and novels.
hogsfm@skynet.be
www.martinrjones.co.uk

Barbara Mariani bb.mariani@libero.it I was born in 1969. I love writing. I've always been interested in literature and it has been my main field of study. I'm so intrigued by the possibility of words to extend and explore the depth and meaning of ourselves and our lives. I graduated after having completed a research study on T.S. Eliot's poem "The waste land". " Never published anything yet, but one day… Who knows? Better give it a try! I'm trying to write fiction, both in Italian and English. As part of my job I do write a lot though. And I know how incredibly important words are… Thanks to BWC for being such a nice gathering of sensitive and gifted people and for giving me an opportunity.

Lida Papasokrati is a medical student and aspiring writer from Greece. Her favourite things in the world include pugs, poetry workshops and anything written by Terry Pratchtett. She currently lives in Brussels, where she only goes on first dates with people who love animals and listen to Dire Straits.

Dimitris Politis was born in Athens, Greece, on 16th of March 1960. He studied Economics at Pireus University in Greece, Classical Studies and Italian language, literature in University College Dublin, and European studies at Trinity College Dublin, in Ireland. He is currently working as Webmaster/Chief Editor of the official European Union website "Europa". Dimitris Politis has published several specialised articles and reviews related to working conditions and health and safety at work in English, Greek and Italian. His first novel "The stolen life of a cheerful man" was published in Greek in Athens on October 2012. Its translation in English came out in late 2014. His second novel "The next stop", also in Greek, is about to be published in Greece in the next months. He has also published several short stories in Greek literary magazines and websites.

Kathleen Reding, as a university professor, published articles in research journals. Now, she has written a children's book about a dog and she is presently working on a memoir. These poems were written during a writers' workshop: frmercure@euphonynet.be

Mauricio Ruiz is a Mexican writer living between Brussels and Oslo. He has published a collection of stories in Spanish entitled *Y Sin Querer Te Olvido,* and is currently working on a novel. He was shortlisted for the 2014 Bridport Prize and is a finalist for the Myriad Books Competition in Brighton, UK.

Klavs Skovsholm was born in February 1963 in Copenhagen, Denmark. He was educated in law at the University of Copenhagen. He has lived in Brussels, for more than twenty years, where he works for the EU. He has published two novels: *Golden Fields* at Balboa Press and *At the Bay* at Partridge. Tel: 02-281-8379 & 0486-582833.

Sabine sur la Lune has been a member of BWC since 2010. She is French and writes in both French and English. Her first professionally published piece was in English: a short comic play for the US magazine "Plays". In the summer 2013, she got married and was finalist in the Wergle Flomp Prize for humour poems, with a poem about marriage. She used the money to buy books about the craft of writing and last year, she finally got published professionally in French for the first time, in the Annual Anthology of éditions Malpertuis. She writes fantasy and is focusing on developing her universe.

Océan Smets started writing and was first published at thirteen. Letters, Poetry, Prose, Poetic prose (Magic Realism), Flash-Fiction. Among his projects a science-fiction novel and a compilation of his experience in a Huron village in Canada. Blog: bligoo.es

Sarah Strange has been writing poems since she was seven. She finds inspiration all around her: nature, people, life events, current affairs, emotions, and the quirky side of life… "Feedback on any particular poem is fun too!" She writes a poem a day. She was published in October 2014. sarah.strange@skynet.be
Skype: wurzel1170 Landline +32 (0) 2 673 28 Twitter @poetinthewoods +32 (0) 474 894 952
BLOG: www.poetinthewoods.blogspot.com

Patrick ten Brink was born in Germany, grew up in Austalia, Japan and England and now lives in Belgium, after some time also spent in France and Mexico. He has published a range of nonfiction books on environmental issues and is currently finalizing the two-part fantasy novel: *The Tides: Accidental Spring* and two travel poetry books: *Galapagos Creatures* and *Memories from Japan*.
www.flickr.com/photos/ptenb
http://allpoetry.com/PatricktenBrink
Patrick_ten_Brink@yahoo.com
www.flickr.com/photos/ptenb
Patrick_ten_Brink@yahoo.com

More books from
Harvard Square Editions: